Wings of Love

SCOTTY CADE

Dreamspinner Press

Published by
Dreamspinner Press
4760 Preston Road
Suite 244-149
Frisco, TX 75034
http://www.dreamspinnerpress.com/

Wings of Love

Cover Art by Braden Williams   http://www.bradenwilliamsromance.com

ISBN: 978-1-61581-731-3

Printed in the United States of America
First Edition
February, 2011

eBook edition available
eBook ISBN: 978-1-61581-732-0

To Kell, my ever-supportive partner of fourteen years. Finding you was my biggest dream come true, but thank you for giving me the time and freedom to chase my other dreams. I love you.

To Joe and Brenda Celeste, whose continued encouragement and support still blows me away. Brenda, you are such a great story developer, and your insight and ability to see right to a character's heart is incredible. Joe, being my heterosexual sounding board during our long cocktail-induced talks on the stern of our boat means more than you can ever know. I love you both.

prologue

RENOWNED oncologist Dr. Bradford Mitchell sat hopelessly in the cold, sterile Seattle hospital room, clinging to the hand of the man he loved more than anything in this world, more than life itself. The man he couldn't save—no matter how hard he tried—from the terrible cancer eating away at his body. As Jeffery Owen, his partner and lover of fifteen years, lay unconscious and seemingly peaceful, Brad watched him draw in and exhale short, steady breaths and listened to the constant *blip-beep blip-beep blip-beep* of the heart monitor, the only sign that Jeff was still alive.

He tried to remember happier times when their lives didn't involve daily doctor's appointments, harsh rounds of chemotherapy, and the many other experimental treatments he'd selfishly forced Jeff to endure. He tried to remember back to when Jeff was a healthy and strikingly handsome young architect with a client list envied by every other architect in his firm. A time when his own thriving practice—now sold—his research, and Jeff were all he needed in this world. They were happy and had the rest of their lives to look forward to.

Then that dreadful day came, with the news of Stage IV colon cancer. Their entire world was turned upside down in one day. After two years of fighting and enduring one experimental treatment after another, Jeff made the decision to stop everything. Brad had tried unsuccessfully to convince Jeff to keep fighting, but Jeff had had enough. Brad knew that the side effects of the treatments were probably worse than the effects of the cancer, at least early on, but he just thought that if they kept trying, something was bound to work. In the end, however, it was Jeff's life and his decision, and like it or not, Brad had to accept it.

Everyone at the hospital knew Dr. Mitch and gave them as much privacy as Jeff's medical needs would allow, which had been a blessing over the last couple of months. Before Jeff slipped into the coma, they'd had long hours just to be together and enjoy the time Jeff had left. Although Brad did his best to hide his breaking heart and grief, he knew Jeff was brutally aware of what he was going through. Jeff had once told him that if their positions were reversed, he couldn't imagine how he would cope. Jeff had done the best he could to prepare and calm Brad, and to assure him that he was at peace with his decision. Jeff had also made him promise to go on with his life, to eventually accept the love and happiness that would surely come his way if he was open to it. He reluctantly promised, as he could never deny Jeff any request no matter how big or small, but he knew the promise was as empty as his heart. He couldn't go on; he couldn't imagine a life without Jeff, nor could he fathom falling in love again.

As Brad sat in the same uncomfortable hospital chair in which he'd sat for the last two and a half months, he didn't feel anything but the empty world around him. Hand in hand and with his head on Jeff's lap and his ear listening to as much as feeling his breaths, he noticed that Jeff's breathing was becoming more and more unsteady and knew that his time on this earth was running out.

Suddenly, as if Jeff were forcing memories of happier times into Brad's defeated body, events of their fifteen years together started to flash before his eyes. The smile on Jeff's face when they together moved into their first home, which he had designed. How every Christmas morning Jeff made them wear goofy flannel pajamas and sit cross-legged around their Christmas tree, opening gifts. How funny Jeff looked at their Halloween party two years ago when he was in a wheelchair and insisted they dress up as Blanche and Baby Jane Hudson from *What Ever Happened to Baby Jane?* How hot he looked in his scuba gear on their last diving trip to Bermuda. How happy and relaxed he was when they were on their yearly trip to Alaska. They'd had such a full, wonderful life, until…. They both thought they had a lifetime together, but fate had other plans. So here they were, Jeff unconsciously fighting for every breath and Brad not knowing which breath would be the last. *God, how did it all come down to this and how will I ever survive?*

Sensing that the end was near, Brad removed his shoes, climbed into the bed, slid his arm under Jeff's neck, and held him close. For the first time since the diagnosis, his tears fell freely. Then the rise and fall of Jeff's chest stopped, and the heart machine indicated a long, flat beep. He closed his eyes, took a deep breath, and calmly reached over and turned off the heart machine. Stone-cold *silence.*

With Jeff still in his arms, he gently kissed him on the lips and whispered, "So long, my love. Rest well." He got out of the bed, picked up his shoes, and backed away from Jeff's bed, never taking his eyes off his lover. When he reached the door, he stood there for what felt like hours; finally he turned and opened the door to what was left of his life.

The next few days were a blur. Friends consoled him, surrounded him, and tried to feed him, but he was just going through the motions. The memorial service and burial were exactly as Jeff wanted, simple and sweet; their friends saw to that. But as he thought back, he couldn't remember a single detail or anything he'd said or anything that had been said to him. All he remembered was seeing a coffin holding the other half of his empty existence.

When the services were over and he'd forced his friends to go home, he was finally alone in the house he and Jeff had lived and loved in. He looked around and immediately knew he couldn't stay in this house any longer, at least not right now. Everywhere he turned, something reminded him of his love and his loss.

Brad spent the next three hours packing his clothes and placed four suitcases at the front door. He wanted to take something to remember Jeff, but what? He took one last look around and decided to take the picture of him and Jeff on one of their many vacations to Hiline Lake in the Alaskan mountains. They both loved the wilderness and especially this spot; they often referred to Hiline Lake as "their spot." They looked so happy then, and that's all he wanted to remember. He put his suitcases on the front porch, called a cab, and closed and locked the front door. He didn't know if he would ever be back, but he knew where he was going.

chapter 1

BRAD arrived at the Seattle airport with no ticket, nor even a schedule of flights to Anchorage. He paid the cab driver, hailed a porter to carry his suitcases, and stood in line at the Alaska Air ticket counter. He bought a ticket on the next flight to Anchorage, where he would charter a floatplane to take him the extra sixty-five miles to Hiline Lake. He had two hours to kill and decided to call a couple of his close friends and let them know where he was going and not to worry, but he didn't know when he would be back. He didn't think he would ever be back, but he wasn't up for lectures about how everything would get better. It wouldn't get better, and he had to find a way to accept and live with that.

His flight to Anchorage was melancholy and uneventful. As they circled to land, he remembered the last time he and Jeff had landed in Anchorage and how happy they were to be on their way to the Alaskan wilderness again. That brought a smile to his face. Upon landing, he hailed a cab to take him to the Lake Hood Seaplane Base, where most of the mountain flights originated. When he arrived, as if on autopilot he walked over to the Trail Ridge Air kiosk, where he spotted a familiar face sitting behind a desk.

Mac looked up in surprise, not expecting to see Brad. McGovern Cleary, Mac to his friends, was the owner and pilot of the one-plane operation that Brad and Jeff had hired on their many trips to Hiline Lake.

The two men embraced, and Mac said, "Well, hey there, stranger. It's been a long time. It's so good to see you, Brad." He looked over Brad's shoulder and asked, "Where's Jeff?"

Brad froze, feeling the blood drain from his face. He had never actually said the words out loud. Mac, sensing something bad, wished he could take back the words immediately, but it was too late.

"Jeff died three days ago, Mac," he choked out.

"Oh my God, Brad. What happened?"

"Cancer," he whispered. "He'd been fighting it for the last year and a half."

"He looked fine the last time you guys were here," Mac insisted.

"Yeah, well, he'd just been diagnosed, and we wanted to make the trip before he started the first rounds of chemotherapy," Brad explained.

"Oh man, I'm so sorry," Mac said. "What can I do?"

"Take me to Hiline Lake," Brad said.

"Sure, Brad, anything. When do you want to leave?"

"The sooner the better. I'm not sure how much longer I can keep it together," Brad said.

"No problem, give me thirty minutes to fuel up and file a flight plan."

"Thanks, man, I really appreciate it."

"Do you have a reservation at the lodge?" Mac asked.

"No, I didn't really think that far ahead," Brad responded.

"Let me call them on their satellite phone," Mac said. "It's been pretty busy up there the past couple of weeks. By the time we get up there, it'll be close to dusk, so I'll need a room too. I'll fly back in the morning."

"Are you sure?" Brad asked.

"I'm sure," Mac said with a weak smile.

Brad waited while Mac made the call. Mac placed the telephone back in the receiver and said, "We're all set. They just had a couple cabins of kayakers check out to do some camping on the lake."

Brad lowered his head as he wiped a tear off his cheek and said, "I don't know how to thank you, man."

"No thanks needed. You'll be okay while I fuel up?"

Brad nodded.

Twenty minutes later, Mac and Brad took off for the forty-minute flight to Hiline Lake. When they landed and taxied over to the plane dock, they were greeted by the lodge owners, Jake Elliot and Alexander Walsh.

Jake and Zander had built the lodge and operated it for the last ten years, and during Brad and Jeff's many visits had developed a casual friendship with them. Luckily, Mac must have informed them of Brad's situation when he called, as they each simply gave him a hug and silently walked him to the lodge.

Before heading to his room, he leaned in toward Mac's ear and whispered, "Thanks for telling them. I don't think I could have handled that again today."

"I figured as much," Mac said. "Listen, if you want to talk tonight or you want to have breakfast with me in the morning, just let me know. Even if you don't want to talk, but just don't want to be alone, I'm here, man, anytime, day or night. I'm in room twelve."

"You're a good friend, Mac. Thanks, man," Brad said.

"I never told you and Jeff this," Mac said, "but my wife died about a year before you started coming up to the lodge, so I know some of what you're going through right now."

"Mac, I'm so sorry. I wish we would have known."

"Nothing you could have done, but I'm glad you know now," Mac continued. "Maybe I can help you in some way."

"I'm not sure anyone can help me, but thanks," Brad said.

"I remember the feeling," Mac replied.

"Thanks again, man. I think I'll head to my room."

Brad started to turn, but Mac stopped him, hugged him, and said, "Try to get some rest."

"I will, thanks," was the last thing Brad said as he walked down the hall and stopped in front of his room. A room that, for the first time in fifteen years, he wouldn't be sharing with Jeff.

chapter 2

BRAD unpacked what he thought he would need for a week or so. He took a long, hot shower and put on his favorite old sweatpants and T-shirt, then sat on the end of the bed. He dropped his head in his hands and, for the second time in three days, let the tears flow freely. He cried until he had no tears left. He sat in one of the two club chairs next to the window and thought about how ironic it was that there would be an empty chair in his life from now on. Then he had to chuckle. *Drama queen*, he thought.

The Alaskan summer days are very long, and it was ten twenty in the evening when he watched the sun drop beyond the mountain range. He and Jeff had watched so many Alaskan sunsets together over the years, from this very lodge, that he almost felt he was cheating on Jeff watching it alone. As the final light faded, he rested his head on the back of the chair and closed his eyes.

When his eyes opened again, it was to a darkened room. He realized he must have fallen asleep, and glanced over at the clock on the bedside table. It was one thirty in the morning; he had slept for five and a half hours, the longest consecutive sleep he'd had in over a week. He stretched and realized his neck was pretty stiff from sleeping in the chair, but he felt okay otherwise. He went to the bathroom, brushed his teeth and combed his hair. He put on a pair of jeans and his sneakers and walked out into the hall. The place was quiet at this hour, and he enjoyed the stillness and peace of the motionless lodge. He walked up and down the halls, then around the grounds until he got cold, realizing he'd left his jacket back in his room. He walked back into the lodge and sat in front of the huge stone fireplace. There was barely any heat radiating, but he was no longer cold. He sat there and stared at the charred wood until the last ember faded away into darkness. He thought about how many times he and Jeff had sat in this very spot and read the newspaper or just talked about their adventure of the day. His bottom lip started to quiver, and he forced the tears back yet again. He got up and walked down the hall toward his room. He didn't know why, but he stopped at room twelve. He raised his hand and lightly knocked on the door. Thirty seconds later, a sleepy Mac stood in the opened doorway in a T-shirt and boxer shorts.

Brad stood there, staring at Mac, not knowing what to say. Mac opened his arms, and Brad fell into them. When the sobs stopped, Brad stepped back and said, "I'm sorry, I didn't know where else to go. I am so tired of crying, but I can't seem to stop."

"You came to the right place," Mac said. "I'm glad you felt comfortable enough to knock on my door. Sit down," he said as he motioned Brad into the room.

Brad sat down in one of the two club chairs that were very similar to the ones in his room. Mac excused himself and went into the bathroom and came out in a pair of blue jeans. When he returned, he sat in the chair opposite Brad and waited for him to speak. Brad took a deep breath and said, "How did you do it? Go on with your life, I mean."

"Well," Mac answered. "When it came down to it, I had two choices. Get out of bed one day at a time and try to put my life back together, or...."

"End it all," Brad added.

"Yeah," Mac said. "To put it bluntly. I thought long and hard about it, and even thought I could pull it off. I'm a pilot, for heaven's sake. It would have been easy. I went as far as taking the plane up and initiating the stall, but in the end I wasn't strong enough to do it and pulled out."

"What made you stop?" Brad asked.

Mac looked out of the large window into the darkness of the Alaskan night and said, "My daughter and a promise."

"I didn't know you had a daughter," Brad said.

"Yep," Mac said. "She's in her second year of medical school back in Seattle. Lindsey and I tried for years to have our own kids, and the doctors finally discovered that I was the problem, so we gave up and adopted Zoe-Grace. She was twelve, and had been in and out of foster care for most of her life, and we thought she deserved a family."

"Good for you, Mac. You must be very proud of her."

"I am indeed, she's a great girl," Mac said.

"I'm sorry for interrupting your story, Mac, please go on."

"Well, near the end, Lindsey made me promise that I would do the best I could to raise Zoe and make a life for the both of us, without her. That conversation kept playing in my head over and over. Even though I'd promised under duress, I still couldn't break my promise to her. In addition, Zoe hadn't had such a great start to life, so it just wasn't fair to her to leave her alone again."

"How did Lindsey die?" Brad asked.

"Breast cancer."

Both men sat in silence for a moment before Brad whispered, "I'm sorry."

"Me too," Mac responded.

They talked until five o'clock in the morning. And although they never acknowledged it, they both knew that a friendship had been forged that would stand the test of time.

chapter 3

LATER that morning the men said their good-byes, and Mac took off for Lake Hood. Brad watched the little plane until it was out of sight, knowing that since Mac exclusively flew all the guests back and forth, as well as weekly supply runs to the surrounding areas, he would see his friend again very soon.

It was a beautiful July summer morning, and the leaves were blowing lazily in the trees. Although he hadn't slept very much the night before, he felt better than he'd expected to. The sweet mountain air and the blue skies did a world of good for his mood, and while he didn't know how long the mood would last, he decided to take advantage of it.

He went back to the lodge and dressed in his hiking gear. He told Jake and Zander that he'd be gone for most of the day, and they offered a brown-bag lunch, which he happily accepted. He started his hike along the lakeshore and headed toward Mount Susitna. He and Jeff had often hiked in the foothills there and had a couple of favorite trails they did each time they vacationed here.

As Brad quietly walked in the sunshine and observed the beauty around him, he felt closer to Jeff than he had at any time in the last few weeks. In Jeff's last days, he'd been in a coma, and although Brad had been happy to be with him, Jeff really hadn't been there. But when they'd been here… Jeff had been so *alive*. The feeling was so overwhelming, Brad suddenly felt weak in the knees. He stopped and sat on a large rock right off the trail and allowed the feelings to take him, harder than ever. Just like that, he was again in a really dark place. Remembering the promise he'd made to Jeff, he forced himself to stand and take a step. *Keep going*, he told himself. *You promised.*

It was about nine thirty in the morning, and he'd been walking for about an hour when he noticed a cabin just off the trail. *I've never noticed that cabin before*, he thought. *But most times we were here in the spring when the leaves were full, green, and vibrant on the trees.* He decided to check it out.

He started off the trail toward the cabin when he noticed a faded old sign covered in brush. He realized he was up in the Alaskan mountains and didn't want to get shot for trespassing, so he thought he should see what it said. He assumed it was a "No Trespassing" or "Private Property" sign, but wanted to make sure. "*Holy shit*," he said out loud. "For Sale."

He felt certain that, since it was for sale—and by the appearance of the sign, had been for quite some time—he could inspect the property without his life being in danger. The approach to the structure was badly overgrown, so it was slow going. He finally reached the wraparound porch and looked up. He grabbed the handrail to pull himself onto the porch, and it promptly came off in his hand. He fell backward and landed square on his butt. Stunned, he sat there for a second, looked up at the sky, and started to laugh. The more he laughed, the louder he got, and his laughter soon became a roar. He knew that wherever Jeff was, he was laughing his ass off too. With a smile plastered on his face, he stood again, and this time with a little more caution, climbed his way onto the porch.

Crossing the porch to the front door, he carefully avoided all the rotten floorboards and reached the door without any mishaps. He felt very silly as he raised his hand and knocked on the closed door. Of course, no one answered, so just for the hell of it, he tried the doorknob. Much to his surprise, the door was unlocked. He opened the door and called out "Hello!" Again no one answered, so he walked in.

The inside was in much better shape than he'd imagined. The cabin was much larger than it appeared from the trail, and fully furnished. It appeared to be one large room, with a loft on one end and an oversized stone fireplace on the other. Under the loft was a small kitchen and what appeared to be a bathroom. He made his way to the bathroom and peeked inside. There was an antique claw-footed tub, an old pedestal sink, and a thronelike thing that said "Envirolet composting toilet." *Yuck*, he thought. *I can't imagine doing my business on that thing.*

He worked his way around the basic kitchen. It had a sink, an old twelve-volt refrigerator, and a wood-burning stove. In the center of the room, in front of the fireplace, was a large couch, two end tables, and of all things, a recliner. Across the room was a bed, dresser, and bedside table. He carefully climbed up the ladder to the loft and found another bed, a chest of drawers, a bedside table, and a blanket chest. Each room had oil-burning wall sconces every four or so feet and an oil lamp on each end table next to the couch and on each bedside table. There was an oil-burning chandelier hanging in the middle of the cabin on a pulley system, which Brad assumed was to raise and lower it for lighting and extinguishing.

On a table to the right of the door was a stack of flyers covered in dust. He picked one up, held it out in front of him, and shook off the dust. The headline read, "Environmentally Green Cabin For Sale." The flyer went on to describe the property in detail. Two acres of natural woodland, twelve hundred square feet, two bedrooms, one bathroom cabin, totally furnished, no electricity, solar panels, twelve-volt battery system, generator, no telephone, well water, and composting toilet. It listed the owner's name and phone number and the price—$69,999.00.

Brad's first thought was, *I'll buy this place. I have no reason to go home, Jeff is gone, my practice is sold, and I'll have plenty to do to keep me occupied. Worst case, if I ever decide to go home, I'll have a cabin to come back to in a place Jeff loved.* It was the quickest decision he had ever made, and somehow he knew it was the right one.

When he got back to the lodge about four o'clock that afternoon, he couldn't believe how energized he felt. He showed Jake and Zander the flyer and told them about his discovery. Much to his surprise, they were aware of the cabin and, of course, knew the owner. They explained that the property was about fifteen miles away by a badly maintained dirt road, but only two or three miles on foot. He told the boys he was going to buy it, and they both looked at him with some resignation.

"Are you sure?" Zander said.

"Yeah, that place needs a lot of work," Jake added.

Before Brad could say a word, Zander piped up again, "That place has no electricity or telephone, and don't even think it has running water."

Finally Brad was able to get a word in. "It has a well with indoor running water. And you're right, no electricity, but solar power, no telephone, and not even cell service, but who do I need to call? And it has plenty of oil-burning lamps."

"Man, you got it bad," Zander said.

"Look," Jake added. "We would love nothing better than to welcome you to our little slice of heaven, but take a while and think about it. Then if you're still serious, you can count on us for all the help and support we can offer, right, Zander?"

"You betcha. But please think about it before you make any quick decisions," Zander added.

"Sorry, Zander, but I've made up my mind," Brad said. "Jeff loved this place, and I feel closer to him here than anywhere else, and right now this is what I need to survive. Can you understand that?"

Certain they wouldn't be able to talk him out of it, they looked at each other, and Zander said, "If this is what you want, you can count on us."

"Thanks, boys," Brad whispered.

The three men hugged, and Brad went back to his room feeling better than he had in any recent memory. Once back in his room, he pulled the flyer out of his pocket and stared at it for a long time. Tomorrow morning he would use the lodge's satellite phone to call the owner and set up an appointment to meet.

chapter 4

THE next morning Brad made the call, and Jake and Zander drove him over to the cabin to meet the owner. He stared out of the window as they drove and thought, *The boys are right. The drive is much longer than the hike, and the roads aren't in the best of shape, but where the hell do I need to drive? Nowhere.* Zander said something to Jake, which interrupted Brad's thoughts, but after Jake answered, there was silence again. In that silence, Brad got lost in his thoughts yet again. *I can spend the entire winter in front of the fire, reading my favorite journals and novels and never see another human being if I don't want to. That's what I need right now, to sort out my feelings and to decide what I want to do with the rest of my life.*

The approach from the road appeared to be kept clear, but everything else was very overgrown. When they reached the porch, the back door was already open, and a tall, thin man with shoulder-length black hair and a long black beard stepped out.

"Hey, Seth," Jake said.

"Jake, Zander, good to see you boys."

Jake said, "Seth Palin, meet Brad Mitchell."

Seth stuck out his hand and said, "Pleased to meet you, Brad."

Brad shook Seth's hand and said "Palin—any relation?"

"Who the hell knows in these parts, but I sure hope not."

Brad smiled and said, "You and me both."

"So," Seth continued, "you think you want to buy this old place, huh?"

"I know I do," Brad responded. "It's exactly what I need right now—a big distraction and a project with no people and no interruptions."

"Hey," Zander and Jake said simultaneously.

"Well, except these guys," Brad said.

"I wrote up an 'Intent to Purchase' last night and hoped this would suffice until I can get back to Anchorage and get you a certified check," Brad said.

"Sure it will," Seth replied. "It's been sitting here for the last several years getting more and more grown over with brush. I just gave up on maintaining it. I've got to tell you, though, what you see is what you get. I won't be fixing anything or guaranteeing anything, either. It is what it is."

"Understood," Brad said. "Now, about the price?"

"Yeah, I know, it's in pretty bad shape," Seth confessed. "What do you say we call it an even fifty grand?"

"Deal," Brad replied. "As long as you show me how to work that throne-looking thing in the bathroom."

"Piece of cake." Seth laughed, and the two men shook on the transaction, both with beaming smiles.

"Hey, Zander," Brad yelled. "When is Mac flying back up?"

"Tomorrow morning. We have two rooms checking in and one checking out," Zander replied.

"Perfect. I'll catch a ride with him to Anchorage, do a little banking, and fly back on his next trip." Brad handed two signed copies of the "Intent to Purchase" to Seth, and Seth signed them both and gave one back to Brad. Just like that, and just like Mac, Brad was on his way to keeping his own promise.

THE next morning, Mac was scheduled to arrive about eight thirty with the expected guests, and Brad was up and dressed. He heard the small floatplane before he saw it and made a beeline to the dock to await its arrival. As Mac circled on his approach, the two exchanged waves, and Brad watched as Mac effortlessly landed the small plane in the middle of the lake and taxied to the dock. After Brad secured the plane, Mac stepped out to help his passengers out of the plane.

"How's it going, Brad?"

"Well, all in all, I think it's going okay," Brad responded. "A great deal has happened since you left. Let's grab a bite of breakfast, and I'll fill you in."

"Sounds like a plan. I'm starving," Mac said.

The two men walked the new guests to the lodge and left them at the front desk in Jake's capable hands. They headed to the dining room, mouths watering for one of Zander's famous Alaskan breakfasts. Jake and Zander noticed that Brad and Mac seemed genuinely happy to see each other, and they were both glad that Brad had someone he felt comfortable enough to confide in.

As they ate, Brad filled Mac in on the cabin purchase and his plans to fly back to Anchorage, do a little banking, and fly back on Mac's next trip. Mac was surprised at this quick decision, and Brad saw the concern in his eyes.

"Mac, I know what you're thinking. I can see that look in your eyes," Brad said.

"This is pretty sudden, Brad," Mac said with an apprehensive tone in his voice.

"I know it is, Mac. And to someone who hasn't walked in my shoes for the last two years, it must seem like the craziest move. When Jeff was diagnosed, I sold my practice and devoted everything I had to helping him beat the cancer, but I failed miserably, and Jeff is...."

Even as he whispered the words, "dead now," they stuck in his throat.

"And besides," he continued, "there's nothing left in Seattle but harsh and sad memories of a life I can no longer have. Sure, we have some great friends in Seattle that were very supportive during Jeff's illness, but the life we shared with them is now over. If they want to see me, they can visit anytime, but I can't go back there, and they'll just have to understand."

"Listen, man," Mac said. "I know it feels that way now, but believe me, in time it will feel different."

"Mac, I know you've been where I am now, but really think back. Honestly, did you believe at the time that things would change, get better?"

Mac thought back to that painful time. "No, I can't say that I did, but I didn't have anyone who had actually experienced what I was feeling to help me through it."

"I know I'm lucky to have you as a friend, Mac, especially since you've experienced the same kind of loss that I just did, but I know I can't go back. And if I can't go back, the only other place to go is forward. I'm asking for your help and support, but if you can't give it, I totally understand." Brad threw his hands in the air. "But either way, I'm doing this. I've made up my mind. Jeff is gone and I made a promise to him, and this is the only way I know how to even start to keep it. I need this, Mac."

Mac sat there, silent, for a few minutes, and the two men simply looked at each other.

"Okay," Mac said. "You've got my support and anything else you need help with."

Brad smiled at Mac and said, "Thanks, man."

"So what's your next move?" Mac asked.

"Well, I've decided to close up our... my... oh hell, the house Jeff and I shared in Seattle and move here full time. I'll need to sink my teeth into the cabin, and when you see it, you'll see why."

"Can we see it this morning?" Mac asked.

"I don't see why not," Brad said. "It's empty and grown over, but not in terrible shape, and in a few days it will be mine." His eyes filled up with tears as he said, "I feel like this is all I have, Mac."

With a knowing look, Mac reached over and, in a show of support, grabbed his forearm and squeezed.

Brad smiled a weak smile and asked, "What time do we have to take off?"

"Checkout time is eleven o'clock, so just after that," Mac responded.

Brad's smile got a little bigger. "I think we have enough time. I'm sure Jake and Zander will let us borrow their truck. If we leave now, we can be back in plenty of time."

Mac stood and said, "Okay then, there's a cabin I want to see."

Ten minutes later, they were on the road.

chapter 5

AS THEY drove along the dirt road in silence, Mac glanced over and saw a hint of a smile on Brad's lips and thought he looked a good bit better than he had when he'd arrived in Anchorage two days before. In all the years since he had met Brad and Jeff, he hadn't noticed how damn tall and broad-shouldered Brad was. His shoulders, along with his tall, muscular frame, seemed to fill up the entire cab of the small truck. Mac suddenly felt guilty that he hadn't offered to drive, as he thought Brad must have felt like he had to fold in half just to fit behind the wheel.

In those earlier years when Brad and Jeff would visit, usually in the spring or summer, he had noticed that they were great-looking guys. He remembered thinking that they were very fit and not the least bit gay-acting, if there was such a thing. All he knew about gay people was what he saw on the news or in some comedy sketch show on television, and that wasn't usually very flattering.

But now, as he looked closer at Brad, Mac noticed how handsome and rugged he was. He had never really noticed what guys looked like on a regular basis, so why now? He was suddenly perplexed and felt himself blush a little. Brad seemed to be built for the wilderness. His straight, blond, shoulder-length hair seemed to frame his rugged face, and why hadn't he ever noticed those deep green eyes? He was hit with a startling thought—*Oh my God, I'm checking Brad out?*

He was shaken out of his thoughts by what he soon realized was a whistle. Brad was whistling. That thought made him relax a little, because until that moment, he hadn't realized just how worried he had been for Brad. He hadn't wanted to show Brad, or Jake and

Zander for that matter, that he was concerned about if Brad didn't start to turn a corner and begin to make peace with his situation, Mac felt Brad would be in real trouble. He'd hoped that Brad would come around, and it appeared that he was starting to do just that.

With Brad's soft whistling steadily filling the little truck cabin, Mac again started to think about his previous realization. *This sudden fascination with Brad has to have something to do with us sharing most of the night talking about and comparing our losses. Maybe it's just part of the bonding process.* Mac thought about how their conversation that night had affected him during his flight home the following morning. He had relived some painful memories of his own, of his beloved Lindsey, but as he always did when his past started to pull at him, he focused on working through the dull pain, and by the time he'd landed, he was back in control. *That must be it. It has to be it,* he thought. *What the hell?* He forced his thoughts back to the cabin. *Could it be the same cabin Lindsey and I had dreamed of buying so many years ago? What are the odds?*

chapter 6

BRAD made a tight right turn and headed up a steep, almost vertical driveway that was bumpy as hell. Again, Mac was shaken out of his thoughts.

"We're here!" Brad said as they climbed their way up the narrow driveway, bouncing around the tiny cab like toy men in a Tonka truck.

"I know the first thing you've got to do after you buy this place," Mac stated.

"What's that?" Brad asked.

"Fix this damn driveway," Mac said with a hint of sarcasm. "If you don't, you'll spend a hell of a lot of money putting shocks and tires on Zander and Jake's truck."

"You're probably right, but don't start prioritizing yet, mister; you haven't even seen the cabin."

Brad pulled the truck up to a huge woodpile at a turnaround and stopped and put the truck in park. They got out and stood for a moment, looking at the back of the cabin. Brad said, "Welcome to Tumbling Downs."

Well, I'll be, Mac thought as he looked at the cabin. "You take me to the nicest places," he said.

"So, whatta you think?" Brad asked.

"Not bad. The way Jake and Zander talked, I was expecting half a roof with no walls. I think this has some real potential."

"Ya think?" Brad asked.

"Yeah, I do, but I'll hold my comments until after the tour," Mac said.

Brad laughed. "I think that's a good idea."

When the tour was complete, they ended up on the front porch, staring out at the spectacular view.

"Okay, so fess up," Brad said. "You haven't said more than three words since we got here."

"To tell the truth," Mac responded, "I'm a little bit jealous. I think I'm in love."

"Hey, hold on a minute, flyboy," Brad said. "I'm nowhere near having a new boyfriend."

With a smirk on his face, Mac said, "Ha-ha, very funny! I was talking about the cabin, you idiot. I'm not buying what you're selling, remember?"

"Yeah, yeah, yeah, that's what all the boys say. So really, what do you think?"

"I really love it. Lindsey and I always dreamed about a little cabin like this, tucked away in the mountains," Mac confessed.

"Well, if you really feel like that, do you want to go in with me?" Brad asked before he had time to think about it. "I'll need a lot of help to put this old place back together."

"Yes," Mac said. "Are you serious?"

"I… I think so." He paused for a minute, and then said, "Yeah, I'm serious. Put it there, partner," and stuck out his hand for a shake. Mac accepted his hand, and with that, they were buying a cabin.

When they got back to the truck, Mac offered to drive back to the lodge, and Brad gladly accepted. The two men talked a mile a minute about all the things they wanted to do and what they should do first and what could wait. The winter would be on them before they knew it, and since Brad was going to live in the cabin through the winter, there were certain things that needed to be taken care of before the first snow. Luckily, there was that huge woodpile, so at least he would be warm.

When they got back to the lodge, they were as giddy as schoolgirls. Jake and Zander couldn't believe the change in Brad in just a few days. The two men shared their news with their friends, and they would have had a beer together to celebrate, but Mac had to fly, and the boys had to work, so they said it could wait until the next time they were all together.

"We better think about getting in the air soon," Mac said.

"When's your next trip back up?" Brad asked.

"Tomorrow," Mac said.

"Okay, perfect. Let me run to my room and get a change of clothes, and I'll be ready to go."

"No problem, I'll take the other guests down to the plane and start my checklist."

"See you in a few," Brad said over his shoulder as he ran back to his room.

chapter 7 ✈

TWENTY minutes later they were in the air and heading back to Anchorage. The noise level in the little plane didn't allow for much conversation, so both men had time to think about what they had just signed up for.

After Mac leveled out at his cruising altitude, his mind began to wander. *What have I just agreed to? I'm investing in real estate with someone I hardly know. I mean, I've flown him—them—back and forth every year for the past five or so years and hung out with them casually at the lodge, but no more than that. What do I know about this guy besides the fact that he's gay and just lost his partner, for God's sake?*

As Brad settled into the co-pilot's seat for the short trip, his mind was doing back flips. *What have I done? I'm buying a cabin with someone I hardly know. Jeff and I hung out with Mac a few times over the years, but I really don't know him very well. Hell, I just found out that he has an adopted daughter and lost his wife to cancer!*

Before either of them could wrap up their thoughts, they were landing at Lake Hood. Mac taxied to the dock, brought the plane to a stop, and said his thanks and good-byes to his passengers. He unloaded the suitcases from the luggage compartment, and everyone was on their way.

It was a little after noon, so Brad had plenty of time to get to the bank and have them cut a certified check. He looked at Mac and said, "Last chance to back out. You were awful quiet during the flight. Are you second-guessing your decision?"

"Hey, you weren't exactly Chatty Cathy either," Mac threw back. "Are you second-guessing your offer?"

Brad laughed. "What do we really know about each other?"

"Not much," Mac said.

"Okay, I don't know why, but I feel very comfortable around you, and although I don't walk around with a tiara on my head all the time, you know I'm gay, and if you don't have a problem with that, then I guess I'm good."

"Well, duh. No one needs to see a tiara on your head to figure out you're gay." Mac chortled.

"Very funny," Brad replied with a smirk.

Mac laughed. "Of course I know you're gay, and I feel pretty comfortable around you, and if you don't have a problem with me being straight, then I guess I'm good too."

"Then it's settled," Brad said.

"I guess so," Mac replied.

They exited the plane and walked toward the terminal.

"I'm going to head out and see if I can grab a cab to the bank," Brad said.

"Not on my watch," Mac replied. "I'll be finished here in twenty minutes, and my truck is in the parking lot."

"This isn't your watch, Mac. You've been great, but at some point you're allowed to be off duty."

"Who says I want to be off duty?" Mac asked. "Who or what do I have to go home to? Zoe's at school and only gets home for spring break and holidays."

"You sure you don't want a break?" Brad asked. "If it makes you feel any better, I'll still be screwed up tomorrow."

"Oh great, a comedian," Mac said. "Give me a few minutes, and we'll head to the bank."

Brad's eyes were filling up again. He stepped up to Mac, threw his arms around the man's shoulders, and whispered, "I really appreciate everything you're doing for me. How will I ever thank you?"

Mac stepped back from the embrace and said, "How about giving me my share of the cabin as a gift?"

"No can do, my friend. You won't really appreciate it unless you pay for it." Brad added, "I'm just looking out for your happiness, you know."

"Thanks a lot!" Mac grumbled.

"No problem, now go get your plane secured so you can take me to the bank."

Mac started walking toward the plane; then he stopped and turned around. "Hey, one more thing. Where are you staying tonight?"

"Oh, no worries, I'll find a hotel nearby," Brad responded.

"No way," Mac said. "I live very close, I have a guest room, and I won't take no for an answer. Besides, we can have that celebratory beer we didn't have earlier."

"I don't know what to say," Brad said.

"Just say yes, and we'll have all the serious stuff settled and be on our way. Remember, since you won't give me my half of the cabin, now I have to go to the bank too."

"Okay, yes!" Brad responded.

"Yes what?" Mac asked.

"Yes, I'll bunk in your guest room. Yes, we can have that beer. And yes, I know you have to go to the bank. Now please get your damn plane secured so we can leave."

"Jeez, you're bossy," Mac shouted, as he started for the plane again.

chapter 8

FIFTEEN minutes later, Mac had the plane secured and they were walking to the parking lot.

"By the way," Mac said, "how much is this little venture going to cost me?"

"A mere twenty-five Gs," Brad replied with a smile.

"Is that all?" Mac said.

"Yep, quite the bargain, don't you think?"

"Sure is," Mac said sarcastically.

They first drove to a branch of Brad's bank, where Mac waited in the car while Brad picked up his check. Then they were off to Mac's bank to do the same. When Mac had his check in hand, they made a quick stop at the package store for some beer and headed to Mac's place.

Mac lived in a trendy suburb called Seward, just outside of Anchorage. The house was a Cape Cod with a white picket fence and a little garage. It reminded Brad of the house in the old television show *Leave It to Beaver*. He didn't quite know what he'd expected, but this wasn't it.

Mac unlocked the front door and, upon entering, Brad saw the house was as charming on the inside as it was on the outside.

He must have had a strange look on his face because Mac said, "Don't look so surprised. Straight men can decorate too."

"Sorry, I didn't know what I was expecting," Brad said. "This is really charming."

"Thanks," Mac replied. "But I was just kidding about straight men decorating. Lindsey did the entire place, and I haven't had the heart to change it. Sometimes it feels like it's all I have left of her, and by changing it, she would be totally gone."

"I can see where you're coming from," Brad said. "I can't even begin to think about our place back in Seattle. I guess I'll deal with it when I'm ready."

"Yeah, you will. Make yourself at home, and I'll open a couple of beers and put the rest in the fridge. The guest room is upstairs, second door on the left, if you want to take your bag up," Mac said.

"Thanks, I'll be right back down."

When Brad came down the stairs, Mac was in the den, starting a fire. "I thought a fire would take the chill off."

"Sure thing," Brad replied. "Can I help?"

"Nope, I got it under control, but thanks."

Brad sat on the couch and took a deep breath, the events of the last few days flooding his mind. Mac finished fiddling with the fire; he kicked off his shoes and sat cross-legged on the opposite end of the couch.

He noticed that Brad suddenly had a somber look on his face and his eyes were starting to fill up with tears. He took a sip of his beer and said, "You okay?"

"I think so," Brad replied. "So much has happened in the last few days. Jeff would have been so excited about this cabin. He loved shit like this."

"Listen," Mac said. "I certainly didn't know Jeff as well as you did, but I've spent some time with both of you, and to be honest, I think he would be very proud of you."

"You really think so?"

"Absolutely."

"Mac?"

"Yeah?"

"Seriously, I don't know what I would have done without you these last couple of days. I mean, I didn't expect this kind of support when I showed up on your doorstep at Lake Hood. I just needed a lift to the lodge."

"I'm glad I could help, and hey, don't forget, I got half a cabin out of it," Mac said through a smile.

They were both startled by the doorbell. Brad wiped his eyes with the back of his hands and said, "I don't care how nice and supportive you are, you're still paying for your half."

Mac got up to answer the door, but said over his shoulder, "Can't blame a guy for trying."

"No, seriously man, thanks," Brad said.

"Anytime," Mac said. "I'll get the door, and you get us another beer, so we can toast to our new adventure."

"Sounds great."

When Brad returned with the beers, there was a really handsome man sitting on the couch.

Mac stood. "Brad, meet Jack Cameron, Lindsey's little brother."

Jack looked to be in his early thirties, with a full head of strawberry blond hair, a fair complexion, and beautiful hazel eyes. Brad stuck out his hand, "Bradford Mitchell, good to meet you."

"Likewise, Bradford," Jack said.

"My friends call me Brad." Brad held out a bottle to Jack. "Beer?"

"Thanks," Jack said.

As Brad headed back to the kitchen to get another beer, he heard Mac say, "You're just in time for the celebration."

"Really, what are we celebrating?" Jack asked.

"My new investment," Mac said. "I am the proud owner of half of an old cabin up at Hiline Lake."

"Wow, congratulations, Mac, I know you've always wanted to do something like this. Am I to assume that Brad owns the other half?"

"Yep. Brad and I met years ago when I would fly him and his partner up to the lake," Mac explained. "His partner recently died of cancer, and he came up to get away for a while, and stumbled onto this cabin. He offered me half, and here we are."

Brad came back from the kitchen with his beer just in time to hear Jack say, "That's great, Mac, I'm happy for you." He turned to Brad and said, "You too, Brad."

The three men held their beer bottles up and touched them together as they all said, "Cheers," and took a swig.

"So, Jackie boy, how's the charter boat business?" Mac asked.

"Pretty good," Jack said. "I've been very busy. In fact, I'm looking forward to a little downtime. I have a week with no charters, so I'm having the boat pulled out of the water to do some maintenance, and I can take a break."

"So what brings you to my neck of the woods?" Mac asked.

"Oh, nothing really. I just wanted to make sure you were okay. I haven't heard from you in a couple of weeks."

"Thanks, Jack, I'm sorry I haven't called," Mac explained. "It's been pretty crazy. I've had flights almost every day and some didn't have any return passengers, so I just stayed at the lake. It saves on fuel, and Zander and Jake are always kind enough to put me up at the lodge."

"You don't have to apologize, Mac. I'm not keeping tabs on you; I was just concerned."

"Hell, Jack, I know that. I'll do a better job of staying in touch, I promise."

"Just invite me up to your new cabin every now and again, and I'll forgive you."

"Deal," Mac said. Then he shyly turned to Brad, looking for some sort of okay from Brad.

Brad nodded in agreement and said, "You're welcome any time, Jack."

They drank the rest of their beer while Mac and Brad told Jack about the cabin, and they discussed what needed to be done immediately and what could wait until the spring. They decided they would check out the solar power system first to make sure it was in good working condition, then the roof, porch, and the plumbing.

While Mac and Brad excitedly discussed their plan of attack, Jack observed the interaction and the relaxed familiar manner between them. *They seem very comfortable with each other*, he thought. *They appear to get along really well, and Mac has needed something like this for a long time. And I'm sure Brad could use a distraction about now. This could be good for both of them.*

Jack stood. "This is all well and good, boys, but I need to get going. I just wanted to check on my favorite brother-in-law."

"Wow. I'm flattered," Mac said. "Although, it would mean a little more if I wasn't your only brother-in-law."

"Very funny, Mac, you know what I mean."

"Thanks, Jack. Let us know when you want to come up to the lake," Mac said.

"Will do, gentlemen—later then?"

"Later," Brad said.

Mac walked Jack to the front door, hugged him good-bye, and closed the door.

He returned to the den and found Brad making a list of things they needed.

Brad looked up. "He seems like a really nice guy."

"Yeah, he saved me when Lindsey died. I'm not sure if I could have gotten through it without him."

"I'm glad he was there for you, and we'll make extra sure we get him up to the lake soon."

"Thanks, Brad, I appreciate that. It means a lot."

"Now let's get to that list."

They continued adding items to the list, such as oil for the lamps, assorted tools, and various supplies. When they were exhausted from all the planning, Mac picked up the remote, turned on the television, and started channel surfing. They settled on *This Old House*, a do-it-yourself home improvement show that was just starting. Talked out, they fell into a comfortable silence.

The next time Brad glanced over at Mac, he was sound asleep with his head back and feet stretched out in front of him, crossed at the ankle. He had never really looked at Mac before, not like this anyway. Mac was really handsome. His jet-black hair, with a little gray at the temples, was the perfect backdrop for his crystal-blue eyes and dimples. He was about five eleven, medium build, with a swimmer's body, lean and fit. He thought back and couldn't remember him and Jeff ever talking about how handsome Mac was; why did they not notice him? Not that it would have mattered; they were a monogamous couple, but every now and then, one or the other would make a comment about another person's looks, just to acknowledge a great body or someone exceptional-looking. Studying Mac now, he could clearly see that he was absolutely gorgeous.

When Brad looked at the TV again, the credits were rolling and he was feeling extremely drained. He reached over and touched Mac on the shoulder and whispered, "Mac, the show's over. I'm going to bed."

"Oh, okay, sorry. I must have dozed off."

"No problem," Brad said. "I'll see you in the morning. And, Mac, thanks again for everything."

"Don't mention it," Mac replied. "Good night, Brad."

"Night, Mac."

Mac stretched as he watched Brad walk up the stairs to the guest room. He felt for the guy. He knew exactly what he was going through, and that made his heart ache for him. He remembered going to bed alone those first weeks after Lindsey died, and the emptiness and loneliness he'd felt. But if he was honest with himself, he also had to admit that he was drawn to Brad in a way he'd not ever experienced with another man. He didn't know if it was because they shared a similar situation—having lost a spouse— or if it was something more.

Mac turned off the television, gathered the empty beer bottles, and put them in the trash. He shut off the lights and started up the stairs. When he got in front of the guest room, he stopped and listened for a second, but heard nothing and continued on to his room. *Good*, he thought. *I hope he's able to sleep.*

Early next morning, Mac was already dressed and sipping a cup of coffee when he heard Brad in the shower. When Brad came down, Mac was pouring him a cup of joe.

"Morning," Mac said. "What do you take in your coffee?"

"Good morning," Brad replied. "Just a little cream or milk, if you've got it."

"Got it," Mac said as he poured some cream into Brad's coffee cup and handed it to him.

"Thanks."

"Sleep okay?" Mac asked.

"So-so. I haven't slept much since Jeff died."

"Yeah, I remember the feeling," Mac said. "And I know you can't imagine it now, but it does get better."

"I'll take your word for it," Brad replied.

"Would you like some breakfast?" Mac asked.

"No thanks, not much of a morning eater," Brad replied. "Coffee's plenty."

"Okay, but you're missing out on my scrambled eggs. I don't like to brag, but they're pretty famous in these parts," Mac said.

"I'll take your word for that too," Brad said as he handed his coffee cup to Mac. "But I will take a refill for the road, if it's not too much trouble."

"No trouble at all. What's the plan?" Mac asked.

"Well, let's see. What time do we need to take off?"

"We need to be ready to go by eleven o'clock," Mac replied.

"Okay," Brad said. "That gives us a couple of hours. I don't have any of my tools here, so do you think we should head to the home improvement store first, get the things on our list and some tools? Or I'm debating if I should fly back to Seattle, get my car and some tools and whatever else we may need."

"You could certainly do that," Mac said. "But think about this: I have every hand and power tool ever made, so we could start with mine, see exactly what we're dealing with, then if we need other stuff and you have it, you could fly back to Seattle and drive it up to Anchorage."

"That sounds like a perfect plan to me," Brad said. "Let's get this show on the road."

And with that, Mac and Brad were on their way. They stopped at the hardware store and then drove right to Lake Hood. The passengers that Mac was flying to the lodge arrived on time, and by ten minutes after eleven, they were in the air.

chapter 9

THEY successfully landed at Hiline Lake on schedule and, as usual, were met by Jake and Zander. The passengers were escorted to the lodge, and Mac and Brad secured the plane. Brad and Mac headed for the cabin to meet Seth. Since there was no mortgage company involved, the closing consisted of a bill of sale and a deed. They met Seth as planned, explained that there would be two buyers instead of one, signed the documents, and gave him the two checks. Within five minutes, Mac and Brad were the proud owners of a new cabin—a fun project for Mac but the start of a new life for Brad.

The two men, happy as clams, went from room to room making notes of what was needed to make repairs and prepare the cabin for the winter. While they worked, they exchanged a comfortable banter about any number of topics, including sports, Brad's naiveté about his first winter at Hiline Lake, and of course, Mac's flyboy attitude about everything. When they were through inspecting the inside, they headed outside to do the same. Besides a few missing roof shingles, some chinking repairs, and rotten floorboards on the porch, the outside of the cabin had held up remarkably well, but the grounds were a different story. The entire two-acre lot was completely overgrown and needed a lot of clearing. They decided to start their attack on the brush and ground cover immediately surrounding the cabin and work their way out from there. Next, they would start topping the trees in front of the porch, which would significantly enhance their one-hundred-and-eighty-degree views. They both agreed that, next spring, there was a lot that could be done to improve the overall look and functionality of the cabin, but they could do it at their own pace.

Once back inside, they took inventory of pillows, blankets, and sheets, then moved to the kitchen and did the same with pots, pans, flatware, dishes, et cetera. Since there was limited electricity, no telephone lines, and no cell phone service, they determined that they would need a battery-operated AM/FM radio, a reliable weather radio, and an AC/DC battery-operated VHF radio. By late afternoon, they felt pretty good about their list and their plan of attack.

"Hey, Brad, you wanna flip a coin for the bedroom?" Mac asked.

"Na," Brad replied. "I hate sleeping in lofts, so the bedroom's all yours, unless you want the downstairs bed."

"Nope, I'll take the loft; I can sleep anywhere," Mac answered.

Brad walked out onto the porch and leaned against the porch rail. He looked off into the distance and thought about Jeff. It had been about three hours since he'd signed the bill of sale and his last thought of Jeff. That was probably a record, and he felt a little guilty. As he stared out into the wilderness at the snow-capped mountains, he wondered what Jeff would think of his decision to buy this place. He was lost in thought when he jumped at the sound of his name.

"Brad! You okay?" Mac asked.

"Oh, sorry, I was just thinking about Jeff and what he would think of this venture," Brad said.

"Well," Mac said, "he loved it up here, and you guys seemed to have a great adventure every time you came, so my guess is that he would be very happy for you."

"You think so?" Brad asked through quivering lips. He turned away just before a single tear slid down his cheek and he began to sob.

"Yeah, I do, Brad."

Suddenly Mac had this overwhelming need to comfort his friend. He reached out, put his arms around Brad, and held him while he cried. When Brad's emotions were under control, Mac released him and began to pull away. In the process, he stopped and looked Brad in the eyes. They held each other's gazes for a moment, and in that instant, Mac saw all the pain and loneliness Brad was feeling. Mac wasn't sure what was drawing him to Brad, but he leaned in and was about to kiss him when, shocked, he caught himself and stopped. Surprised by his desire, he immediately pulled away, shook his head, and walked back into the cabin.

What the hell was that? he thought as he sank down on the couch. *One minute I was reassuring the guy, and the next I was about to kiss him. Where in the hell did that come from?*

chapter 10

BRAD stood frozen and alone where he and Mac had embraced just moments ago. Until Mac, red-faced and notably shaken, had abruptly turned and walked into the cabin. *Was Mac about to kiss me? No, it must be my imagination. Mac is straight. I need to get a grip. He was just being supportive.*

Brad took a few more minutes to get it together and walked into the cabin. Mac was sitting on the couch, still looking a little nervous.

"Hey buddy," Brad said. "I'm starved. What say we head back down to the lodge, grab an early dinner, get a good night's sleep, and get an early start tomorrow?"

"Sounds like a plan," Mac replied. "I don't have passengers to take back tomorrow morning, so we can leave as early as we want to."

Brad and Mac closed up the cabin and drove back to the lodge. They ordered burgers and beer and made their plan of attack for the next day. They would fly out at first light, head over to Mac's house, and while Brad went to the home improvement store, Mac would pack up all the tools he thought they might need. If all went as planned, they would land back at the lake by two o'clock, and after unloading and securing the plane, be at the cabin no later than three o'clock.

When the food came, they ordered another round of beer and ate mostly in silence. Brad thought that Mac seemed a little nervous and uncomfortable, but didn't want to say anything in case he was simply imagining it. When they finished eating, Mac stood and said, "I'm beat, I think I'll turn in. How about we take off around eight?"

Brad stood as well and said, "Sure, eight's fine. Good night, Mac, see you in the morning."

"Good night," Mac said with a halfhearted smile, and he turned and walked away.

Brad watched Mac until he disappeared around a corner. He knew he wouldn't be able to sleep, so he sat back down and ordered another beer.

While he drank his beer, he kept replaying that strange embrace in his mind. Mac had hugged him once or twice since he'd showed up at the lake, but this embrace had felt different somehow. The look in Mac's eyes had been so intense and the way he'd pulled back so quickly and fled…. *Is Mac struggling with something?* Brad tried to come up with a scenario that might explain Mac's behavior. *Maybe while trying to comfort me, he was reliving his wife's death.* After all, they'd been through the same experience, losing their spouses. That's got to be it. *How could I have been so selfish? I never once thought about how he must be feeling, going through this with me. I'll do better tomorrow. No more breakdowns in front of him. No more sad stories.*

Brad downed the last of his beer and headed to the front desk. Before he got there, he ran into Zander in the hall, so he told him that tonight would be his last night at the lodge, as he planned on moving into the cabin tomorrow, and he needed to settle his bill. Zander congratulated him again on the purchase as they walked together to the front desk. He assured Brad that they would see a good bit of each other in the future.

Brad made his way to his room, packed his bags, took a quick shower, and crawled into bed. He read until he got sleepy and then turned out the light. As he drifted off to sleep, his last thoughts were of Jeff.

MAC lay awake in bed, tossing and turning, getting more frustrated by the minute. After an hour of trying to fall sleep, he finally gave up. He got out of bed, got a drink of water, sat in the chair, turned on the reading light, and opened a book. He was reading the same paragraph for the third time when he heard a door close. His room was right next to Brad's, so he knew it was Brad turning in. He closed his book and rested his head on the back of the chair. His thoughts went immediately back to Brad. *Man, I hope he didn't realize I was about to kiss him. Oh crap, I almost kissed him.* He had never consciously thought about Brad in that way—not any guy, for that matter—but it was hard to deny the instant need he'd had to take the pain away when he looked into Brad's eyes.

Okay, Mac, your brain is on overload. You can't keep this up. You need sleep. Besides, it was probably a one-time thing anyway. Quit overanalyzing. You just hopped onto the emotional rollercoaster that Brad was on. It wasn't that long ago when you were on the same ride. You remember what is was like, and you were just reacting, that's all.

Hoping like hell his rationalization worked, he turned off the reading light and got back into bed for the second time in one night. He decided then and there that he wasn't getting up again, and damn it, he was going to sleep. And he did.

chapter 11

AT SEVEN o'clock the next morning, Mac walked into the dining room and was greeted by a smiling Brad, sitting at the breakfast table and sipping a cup of coffee.

"I was wondering if you were ever going to get up," Brad said.

"Good morning to you too," Mac replied. "And just for the record, it's only seven o'clock."

Smiling, Brad said, "I've been up since four o'clock. It's a beautiful morning and looks like great flying weather."

"Are you always this chipper in the morning?" Mac asked.

"Nope, I'm pretty subdued this morning."

"Oh man, thanks for the warning," Mac shot back.

Zander came out of the kitchen carrying a pot of hot coffee.

"Morning, Mac," he said from the swinging doors.

"What does a guy have to do to get some breakfast around here?" Mac asked.

"Order it," Zander said.

"Fine," Mac said. "Why does everyone have to be a comedian?"

Zander nudged Brad's shoulder and said, "Somebody woke up on the wrong side of the bed this morning, yeah?"

"Looks like it." Brad chuckled.

Mac ordered his breakfast, and Brad had another cup of coffee. The guys went over their plans once more and headed back to their rooms to get their stuff.

Mac and Brad met at the front desk, where they turned in the keys and said their good-byes to Jake and Zander. Moments later they started for the dock where the plane was tied up.

"Mac?" Brad said.

"Yeah, Brad?"

"Can I talk to you about something?"

"Sure," Mac said.

"About last night," Brad started.

Mac mentally froze. *Here it comes. I'm so busted*, he thought.

Brad continued, "I really appreciate your support, now and when I showed up here out of the blue. In many ways, I would have been lost without you taking me under your wing. But I think I owe you an apology."

"What for?" Mac asked hesitantly.

"Well, I think I was so wrapped up in my own pity party that I never thought about how my situation might bring back a lot of raw memories for you. Last night, after I broke down yet again and you helped me through it, I looked at you and saw a lot of pain and confusion in your eyes. That's when it hit me. I just wasn't thinking clearly, and I'm really sorry."

By this time they had reached the plane. Mac put down his bag and released the breath he didn't realize he was holding. He turned to face Brad.

"Look, Brad, you don't owe me an apology. Sure, your situation brings back some painful memories for me, but I'm strong enough now to handle them. I've had many years to adjust to Lindsey's death, and I've made my peace with it, just as you will with Jeff's death."

"Thanks for saying that, Mac, but I just want you to know that I'm going to do a better job at pulling myself together."

Mac opened his mouth to speak, and Brad put his hand up.

"Don't say anything, Mac. Please let me finish. First of all, no one wants to listen to my sad stories all the time. Secondly, it's time that I accept that Jeff is gone and start to deal with it. Yeah, I miss him, and it's really tough, but I feel the closest to him here, and I am especially grateful for your friendship."

Brad stepped closer to Mac and put both arms on Mac's shoulders and whispered, "I'm going to get my act together, I promise."

Where Mac had seen pain and hurt in Brad's eyes last night, this morning he saw hope and gratitude. He couldn't help himself; he pulled Brad into a hug and slapped his back a couple of times, then stepped back and said, "You're welcome. Now can we just go? All this girl talk is making me uncomfortable."

"You're a butthole," Brad said with a sneer. "Let's get this damn show on the road."

Brad had helped Mac get the plane ready to go several times now, so they fell into an easy routine. As Mac went through his checklist, Brad loaded the bags into the rear compartment and started to untie the lines securing the plane to the dock. They finished about the same time, and Mac climbed in and started the engine. When the engine was warmed up, Brad untied the last remaining line, stepped on the pontoon, and hopped into the cockpit. He secured the door as they taxied into the middle of the lake and lifted off.

It was an exceptional morning. The sky was bright blue, the air was smooth, and visibility was perfect. As usual, the noise in the cockpit didn't allow for much conversation, and Mac was on the radio with the tower at Lake Hood on and off, changing routes and altitudes, so Brad sat back and enjoyed the flight. Fifty-five minutes later, they were on the ground in Anchorage. They secured the plane to the dock and headed for Mac's truck. Brad drove and dropped Mac off at his house to start gathering tools, while he headed straight for the home improvement store. While en route, Brad had an astonishing thought: *How are we going to use power tools?* There was only limited solar power and a small generator to charge the battery packs in the event of no sun. *This wilderness thing is going to take some getting used to,* he thought. *I'll buy another larger generator for the power tools, and as long as I have the generator, why not buy a microwave oven? That'll come in handy for my microwave popcorn, and oh, maybe an electric coffeemaker.*

Brad was still laughing at himself while he loaded the generator, microwave oven, and electric coffeemaker into the truck, along with the rest of the supplies he'd purchased. When he got back to Mac's, there was a pile of hand and power tools in the driveway, along with six grocery bags, and Mac was coming out of the house with a cooler.

Brad still had a smile on his face as he got out of the truck.

"What are you smiling at?" Mac asked.

"How do you think we'll use these power tools at the lake?" Brad asked.

Mac looked perplexed. "Damn, you're right, limited electricity," he said.

"I am right," Brad replied. "But I had an epiphany en route. Take a look in the back of the truck."

Now Mac had the same smile on his face that Brad was sporting.

"Smart man," Mac said as he caressed the generator. "I see you've added a few other creature comforts of home as well," he said, referring to the microwave and coffeemaker.

"Yeah, you got a problem with it?" Brad asked.

"Nope, I got no problem with it. I'm as spoiled as the next guy." Mac chuckled.

They loaded the rest of the tools in the truck and drove back to the airport. Mac pulled the truck right up to the dock, so they could load the plane. While Brad unloaded the truck, Mac carefully weighed each tool before loading it into the plane to make sure he didn't go over his weight load. Within an hour, they were back in the air, and Brad was on his way to his new life.

chapter 12

THEY landed at the lake as planned, unloaded and carried everything up to the lodge, and borrowed and reloaded Zander and Jake's old pickup truck. They took a break and grabbed a quick bite. When they were finished eating, they again went over their supply list to make sure they hadn't forgotten anything. Soon the two men were bouncing around the cab of the little truck, making their way to the cabin.

When they reached their destination, they unloaded the haul for the last time and took the truck back to the lodge. Jake offered to bring them back to the cabin, but it was only three thirty and the weather was still beautiful, so they opted to hike and enjoy the weather while they still could. Winter would be moving in soon enough, and days like this would be hard to come by.

They reached the cabin just after five o'clock, giving them approximately five hours of daylight remaining. This was going to be their first night in the cabin, and since they had no idea what to expect, they really needed a game plan. Mac reached into the cooler and pulled out two beers, and they headed out to the porch, careful to avoid the rotten floorboards. With pen and pad in hand, they made a list of things to do before nightfall. When the list was complete, they set out on their chores with a vengeance. The first order of business was to make sure all the oil lamps were full and the wicks were in good working order. Then they stocked the huge wood compartment built into the stone fireplace with as much wood as it would hold. Winter was still officially four or so months away, but in the summer, it could drop to the upper thirties at night, and they wanted to be prepared. Next, Brad made the beds with the linens Mac had packed and made sure each bed had extra blankets, while Mac made sure the water reservoir was full and the hand water pump was primed. Mac noted that they would need to make sure the wood-burning stove was hot, to boil some water for baths later that night. They busied themselves around the cabin until the sun was about to set. They opened another beer, headed to the porch, and made a toast to their first day as they watched the sun fall behind Mt. Denali. Five minutes later, both men were again busy as bees. Brad lit the oil lamps as Mac tackled the chandelier. Brad commented that the cabin took on a nice glow as the shadow of the flames danced on the log cabin walls and ceiling, but they had no time to watch; there was more work to be done. The kitchen needed to be thoroughly cleaned, as did the bathroom, and they hadn't even thought about dinner.

While Brad cleaned the kitchen and bathroom, Mac set up the generator on the back porch and filled the fuel tank. He ran a multi-outlet extension cord through the window and plugged in the microwave and coffeemaker. With that done, thinking ahead, he scanned the cabin; next to the wood-burning stove was a large tub, which he assumed was for heating water. He intently studied the old stove until he thought he had figured out how the thing worked. He opened the door to the compartment on the left, and from the pile of ashes he saw, he assumed that section was the wood box. He loaded some kindling and a pile of logs into the compartment and lit the kindling and nursed the fire until it caught. He closed the firebox door, filled the tub with water, covered it, and placed it on top of the stove. Feeling pretty good about himself, he moved on to his next chore, which was to light a fire in the old stone fireplace. They hadn't tried it yet and hoped it still had a good draw—or they might just freeze this winter—but when he opened the damper and felt a breeze, he knew the chimney wasn't clogged. He lit the fire, and to his amazement, it all worked perfectly. He stoked the fire and turned to put the iron tool on its rack. That's when he caught a glimpse of Brad coming out of the bathroom. He howled with laughter. He laughed so hard he barely caught his breath.

"What's so funny?" Brad asked, not knowing why Mac was hysterical.

"Have you looked at yourself in the mirror lately?" Mac asked.

"No, why?"

"Just do it," Mac instructed.

Brad went back into the bathroom and looked at himself in the mirror. He began to roar with laughter himself as he saw his reflection in the mirror. He had a blue bandana tied around his head, and it was soaked through and through with sweat or soapy water, he didn't know which. His face, neck, and sweatshirt were covered with dirt, his hands were in yellow rubber gloves, and he was holding a mop and bucket. He thought he looked just like his grandmother's old cleaning lady.

Mac joined him in the bathroom, and they both chuckled while Brad tried to wash the dirt off of his face.

"Man, this place must have been really dirty," Brad said. "Look at me. I'm a mess. I scrubbed that old tub so hard I was afraid I'd scrub the porcelain right off."

"You did a great job," Mac replied. "It looks clean as a whistle."

"Thanks," Brad said.

Suddenly they heard a loud rumble, like someone was holding a sheet of tin and moving it back and forth to imitate thunder. They both looked in the direction of the noise. Their eyes grew wide with amazement as flames shot out of the top of the stove; the old aluminum tub and lid were bouncing around like they would both fly off of the stove at any minute. Brad saw Mac run toward the stove, but before he could say anything, Mac quickly grabbed the lid handle and lifted it off of the tub. He howled in pain and dropped the cover onto the floor.

"Damn it," he yelled. "How did it get so hot so fast?" He grabbed the wrist of his burned hand with his other hand and stared at it in shock. "I just put the water on ten minutes ago."

Flames were still shooting out of the top of the stove, so Brad quickly filled a bowl with water, used a wet towel, opened the firebox door, and threw the water in. The stove began to sizzle and the flames quickly turned to smoke. Brad pushed Mac toward the door, and when he was safely outside, Brad ran back in and began to open the back door and the windows. When every door and window was open, he quickly found his medical bag and a flashlight and headed for the porch.

"How bad is it, Mac?" Brad asked.

"I don't think it's too bad," Mac replied. "I released the lid pretty quickly."

Brad handed the flashlight to Mac and said, "Let me take a look." Mac took the flashlight and shined the light on his burned hand.

Brad took Mac's hand, careful not to touch the burned area, and examined it. It was a relatively small first-degree burn across the center of his hand and in the crease of his fingers, where he'd grabbed the lid handle.

"Stay put," Brad said as he went back into the cabin. He was back in less than a minute with a bowl of warm water he'd made by scooping a cup of boiling water from the tub and mixing it with the cool water from the well tap.

He was just starting to clean the burned area with the warm water when Mac asked, "Shouldn't we put butter or something on it?"

"Nope," Brad responded. "An old wives' tale—butter's not good for burns." Brad then cringed and said, "This might hurt a little," as he tried to get Mac's wedding ring off of his hand. Mac looked very concerned.

"Why do we have to take my ring off?" Mac asked.

"You might have some minor swelling or edema, and I don't want the ring to cut into your finger," Brad said.

"You think it's that bad?" Mac asked.

"No, I don't, but I'd rather be safe than sorry."

Mac was sitting on the floor of the porch with his legs crossed, Indian style, and Brad was in the same position right in front of him. Mac leaned back against the wall of the cabin, laid his head back, and closed his eyes as Brad finished dressing the wound. Mac tried to relax his breathing and concentrate on keeping still and not jerking his hand away as Brad took care of the burn.

When he was relaxed and clam, Mac realized that Brad was caressing his hand and gently cleaning the burns, and it felt kind of good. The way he was stroking the burn, it was almost sensual, and although he was sure Brad didn't mean it in that way, it felt really erotic. Mac panicked when he realized his dick had jumped to attention. He certainly didn't want to alert Brad to this sudden interest, so he tried to casually change positions so Brad couldn't see the bulge in his pants.

When Brad had finished dressing the burn, Mac quickly stood and walked around the porch with his back to Brad.

"Thanks, Brad," Mac said. "Let's go check out the mess in there and see what we need to do about it."

"You stay out here for a minute, and I'll go check on the stove," Brad said.

When Brad got inside, most of the smoke had cleared and he could see that the fire was out in the stove. He used the fire tools near the stove and cleaned out the firebox, loaded a small log and some kindling, and lit the fire again.

Mac came in and said, "I'm really sorry, Brad. What did I do wrong?"

"I think you just put too much wood in the firebox, that's all."

"Oh, is that all," Mac said as he laughed. "I could have burned this place to the ground."

"No harm done," Brad said. "Listen, it's getting pretty late, and this water is still really hot, so I'm going to dump it in the bathtub, and you can get cleaned up, while I boil a little more for me. But be careful and try not to get your bandages wet."

"Why don't you go first, and I'll get these windows and doors closed. It's getting pretty chilly in here," Mac said.

"Nah, you go," Brad said. "I'll do all of that. Besides, I think I'll soak a while when it's my turn, and I'll feel rushed if you haven't had your bath, okay?"

"Okay," Mac mumbled.

While Mac got a change of clothes and his toiletries, Brad carried the tub over to the bathroom and poured the hot water into the bathtub. He was turning on the tap when Mac walked in carrying a black leather bag and wearing only his boxers and a T-shirt.

"You're on your own," Brad said. "Just make sure you test the water before you get in. That water was boiling when I took it off of the stove. I don't want to have to grease your entire body down with burn ointment."

"Ha-ha," Mac said sarcastically and rolled his eyes. "I heard you doctors were assholes, but I didn't believe it until today."

Brad chuckled. "You haven't seen anything yet."

"Hey, Brad, do you have my wedding ring?"

"No, I put it on the kitchen table," Brad said.

"No problem, I'll get it."

When Mac came back with the ring in his hand, he could see the questioning look in Brad's eyes.

"This is the first time I've taken this ring off since Lindsey put it on sixteen years ago."

"Wow, Mac, I'm sorry. I should've realized that when I saw you were still wearing it."

"Not your problem, Brad. I'm a big boy, I could've said no. Maybe it's time."

"You know, Mac, you didn't take the ring off, I did. So technically you still haven't taken it off."

"I guess you're right," Mac said. "But I think the time is right. I can't preach to you about moving on with your life if I can't do the same. So, a new start for each of us."

Brad smiled and said, "A new start."

"Brad?"

"Yeah."

"Get out of here so I can take a bath," Mac said.

"Oh, sorry."

Brad stepped out of the bathroom and closed the door behind him. He proceeded to close all the windows and doors. He walked to the kitchen and grabbed a bottle of red wine, two glasses, and a corkscrew. He picked up an oil lamp from the end table and walked out onto the porch. It was cool and crisp, but not too cold yet. He sat on the floor and leaned against the wall. *We need to get some porch furniture*, he thought. He opened the wine bottle and poured himself a glass. His second thought was, *Did Mac have a hard-on when I was bandaging his hand? I think he did. I think I know a hard-on when I see one. Besides, his cargo pants looked like a circus tent.* He took another sip of wine.

He heard the screen door open and close, and he looked up to see Mac dressed in long flannel pajama pants, a sweatshirt, and heavy wool socks, his wet hair slicked back. *He looks like an Abercrombie & Fitch model*, Brad thought.

"How was the bath?"

"Quick, but hot," Mac responded.

"How's the hand?"

"Okay," Mac said. "I think I managed to keep the bandage dry."

"Good, tomorrow morning I'll redress it and take another look."

"Thanks, Brad."

"No problem." Brad downed the last of his wine and refilled his glass. He poured a glass for Mac and handed it to him as he stood. "My turn for a bath. See you in a bit."

Brad left Mac standing on the porch and made his way to the kitchen. He again removed the tub of hot water from the stove, carried it to the bathroom, and poured the water in the tub. He turned on the cold tap, returned the tub to the kitchen, and slipped back into the bathroom. He undressed, tested the water, and slipped into the hot water. He quickly sighed as he noticed how comfortable the tub was. It was long enough to stretch out, very deep, and tall enough on one end to comfortably lean back and rest his head and neck while most of his body was covered in the water.

He totally relaxed and let the hot water consume him. Steam was rising off of the water, and through the steam he could see the flickering flame from the oil lamp casting an eerie glow. He watched the flame dance on the ceiling, and for the first time in ages, he felt totally relaxed. He thought about how a hot water heater and shower would make things easier at bath time and decided that he was going to talk to Mac about upgrading the solar electrical system to allow for the extra power they would need for a few modern-day necessities. He took another sip of his wine and put the glass on the floor next to the tub. He laid his head back and closed his eyes. His thoughts went to Mac. *Mac seems to be having some very odd reactions to me. The almost-kiss. The hard-on. And sometimes I catch him staring at me from a distance. Could Mac be struggling with his sexuality? Just because he was married doesn't mean he's straight, but never in all the years we've been coming up to the lake did we ever get a vibe that he was gay. If he's struggling, I need to help him.*

chapter 13

WHILE Brad was having his bath, Mac stood leaning on the porch railing, looking up at the dark blue velvet sky. He was always so amazed at how close the stars appeared to be when he was up in the mountains, like he could reach out and touch them. He and Lindsey had loved stargazing. They would lie on a blanket in their backyard and look at the stars for hours. "Lindsey, I miss you so much," he said under his breath. Then his thoughts took over. *Why am I having these feelings for Brad? I'm not gay. My God, I got a woody when he was dressing my burn. I've never been attracted to another guy, but these thoughts are pretty hard to deny. What do I do?*

He was startled out of his thoughts by a hand on his shoulder.

"Mac, are you okay?" Brad asked.

"Oh yeah, why?"

"I called your name twice, and you never heard me."

"I'm sorry, I was thinking about Lindsey. We loved the stars, and they are so vibrant tonight," Mac said.

"They are indeed—so close, yet so far," Brad whispered.

"Bath okay?" Mac asked.

"Really good; I was so relaxed I dozed off for a few minutes."

"Speaking of sleep, I'm pretty tired as well. Why don't I make us a quick bite, and we can turn in?" Mac said. "We have a big day tomorrow."

"Sounds good, can I help?" Brad asked.

"Sure. How about I make a couple of sandwiches and you toss a salad?" Mac said as he opened the cabin door.

"You got it," Brad replied.

Mac walked into the cabin with Brad behind him. They prepared their dinner and ate mostly in a comfortable silence, both seemingly lost in thought. When they were through eating and everything was clean and put away, Mac folded the dishtowel and threw it over the edge of the sink.

"I guess that does it," Mac said. "I think I'll turn in."

Their eyes met for a brief second and lingered. Brad said, "Okay. Good night, Mac."

"Sleep tight Brad," Mac responded. He climbed the ladder to the loft, pulled back the covers, and slipped into bed. Brad threw a few more logs on the fire, and put out all the oil lamps.

"Hey, Mac?" Brad shouted.

"Yeah, Brad?"

"I'll keep the fire going tonight. No need for you to go up and down the ladder in the dark."

"Okay, thanks, I'll take it tomorrow night," Mac responded.

Brad made his way to his bed by the light of the fire, and crawled in. The cabin was silent except for the crackling sound of the wood burning. The sound was soothing, and he fell asleep immediately.

Unfortunately for Mac, sleep didn't come. He went over and over the events of the day, the last couple of weeks, and the last five years since he and Brad had met. When they'd first met, Brad was with Jeff. Lindsey had just died, and Mac wasn't interested in anything but trying to get through a day. And he was straight; what part of being straight had he forgotten? But how could he explain the feelings for Brad he was experiencing? He thought back to high school. He had experimented with a couple of guys while he was on the swim team, but hadn't every guy at that age? It was enjoyable, sure, but he never thought it would ever go beyond just that, two guys getting their rocks off. He had never ever remembered consciously being attracted to another man. *Could it be that I've denied that part of myself for all these years?* Question after question popped into his mind.

This attraction couldn't be real; it had to be something else. He again thought of Lindsey. *I can't betray her with a man. I know she wanted me to move on and find love again, but I'm pretty certain she didn't mean with a man. And besides, Brad just lost Jeff. The last thing he needs is a straight man coming on to him. What am I saying? I'm not going to hit on Brad. I'm straight!*

Mac grabbed his head with both hands and squeezed his eyes shut. His brain was again on overload. He needed to stop stressing over this infatuation. Winter would be here soon, he would see a lot less of Brad, and whatever he was feeling would just go away. He convinced himself to give it up, hold up his end of the bargain where the cabin was concerned, and pray that winter came very soon.

chapter 14 ✈

TIME was flying by. They were so busy with the cabin that Halloween and Thanksgiving had come and gone almost unnoticed, and it was now early December. Over the last six months, the two men had fallen into a fairly easy routine. Mac had done his best to deal with his infatuation with Brad by flying as much as he could and staying in Anchorage as much as possible without making Brad feel deserted. After all, he'd gone into this partnership with open eyes, and it wasn't Brad's fault he had issues. He owed it to Brad to pull his share of the workload. Most days he would fly his passengers to and from the lodge and pick up supplies, while Brad stayed behind and worked on smaller projects. When Mac had a day or two off, they tackled the larger projects together.

The day after Mac had burned his hand boiling water, they decided to make the upgrades Brad had thought about. They had the cabin rewired for an updated solar power grid that would accommodate a solar water heating system, a refrigerator, and a small washer-dryer combo. At the same time, they had the old generator rebuilt and rewired to come on automatically when the batteries on the new solar grid needed charging or if they simply needed a power boost. They also had the cabin's plumbing updated to accommodate a shower and hot running water.

All the repairs were complete. They had hot water, more electricity, and enough wood chopped, split, and stacked to heat the cabin through the winter. Once winter set in, Brad knew that Mac would only be able to fly up weather permitting, so he made sure the cabin was stocked with nonperishable foods for the long stretches of bad weather.

Zander and Jake had decided to close the lodge for a week to visit family, and for the last week or so, they had buttoned up the lodge and prepared it for their time away. Mac had been up at the cabin with Brad during that time, tackling the chinking repairs needed on portions of the log cabin walls. It took them almost the entire week, but they were finally finished. When the workday was over, they sat in their new rocking chairs on the porch to have a glass of wine. With the trees now topped and the brush cleared, the view was even more spectacular than before. Not only could they clearly see the majestic mountains in the distance, they had a clear shot down to the lake and could see the lodge and the dock where Mac kept the plane.

Brad poured a glass of wine for Mac and poured one for himself. They rocked slowly as they looked out at the mountains. "Man, the view is spectacular now, isn't it?" Mac asked.

"Hell yeah," Brad said. "The mountains and the lake seem so close."

"I love being able to see my plane," Mac said. He looked over to the north and commented on how the clouds were starting to roll in.

Earlier in the day, Brad turned on the weather radio to get an update and learned that the first big winter storm was scheduled to arrive in three days. The blizzard was expected to drop as much as three to four feet of snow, with whiteout conditions and fifty- to sixty-knot winds.

Mac was flying Zander and Jake to Anchorage to start their vacation in two days and wouldn't be back until the storm broke, which meant Brad would be alone in the cabin during the first storm of the winter season.

He was a little nervous, but when he thought about it, if he were being honest with himself, it had more to do with Mac leaving than the storm approaching. He had grown accustomed to being with Mac off and on over the last six months, but this past week or so with Mac was the happiest he'd been since Jeff died. They had discovered that they really had a lot in common. They liked the same sports teams, enjoyed many of the same foods, read many of the same books, and shared a love for adventure and, oddly enough, microwave popcorn. They had easily made their own place in the cabin and felt comfortable doing so. Many times they would sit in front of the fire with their feet up and read in a comfortable silence while chomping on their favorite snack. Or sometimes Mac would head up to the loft and read alone, or Brad would sit on the porch and read until the sun went down. But they both knew the other was just a call away, and there was a certain comfort in that. Through the pain of losing Jeff and buying and restoring this cabin, Brad had found a best friend for life.

After they finished their wine, they started the nightly drill. Although they now had electricity, they still liked to use the oil lamps as much as possible. Brad lit the oil lamps while Mac got the fire going in the large fireplace. Together they moved effortlessly around the little kitchen, cooking dinner and listening to the weather radio.

When dinner was ready, they ate at the kitchen table, as they did most nights, and talked about the storm and what they needed to do to prepare. They had one more day to secure the cabin before Mac flew back to Anchorage.

After they'd finished eating, and they were satisfied with their plan of attack for tomorrow, and the kitchen was cleaned, they each grabbed a book and headed to the couch. They read for a couple of hours in silence.

Brad closed his book, stretched, and said, "Mac?"

Mac looked up and closed his book.

"You never talk about your family other than Zoe-Grace," Brad said. "Do you have any brothers or sisters? Are your parents still alive?"

Looking a little uncomfortable, Mac closed his book and looked at the ceiling.

"What I know is a really short story," Mac said. "I didn't know either of my parents. I was told that my mother became pregnant with me while she was still in high school. She was forced to give me up for adoption by her parents, my grandparents, and I spent seventeen years in orphanages and foster homes."

"That must have been tough," Brad said.

"I survived." Mac replied as he shrugged his shoulders.

"Do you have any siblings that you are aware of?" Brad asked.

"About ten years ago, I found out that I have a half sister, to whom I'm not very close, and she also has a daughter."

Mac sat up and smiled warmly. "But to be honest, the only family I've ever known is Lindsey's family. When we got married, they accepted me with open arms and made me feel like I'd been in the family as long as Lindsey had."

Then his smile faded as quickly as it came. "Her father died of a heart attack a year before Lindsey died, and her mother died of breast cancer three years ago. Jack, Lindsey's only brother, whom you've already met, was married and divorced at a very young age and didn't have any children. So, Jack and Zoe are the only family I have, and we're pretty close."

"Wow," Brad said. "That's some story. I'm really sorry, Mac. It couldn't have been easy growing up in those conditions."

"It was all I knew," Mac replied. "But from a very young age, I figured out I had two choices. I could take the high road, work hard, make do, and survive. Or I could take the low road and probably end up dead or in prison."

"Seeing the man you've turned out to be, I can clearly see what road you chose," Brad said with admiration.

By now, Mac was pacing in front of the fireplace, clearly not comfortable talking about himself, but fully committed to telling his story.

"Yep, I chose the high road, and as soon as I was old enough to work, I saved every penny I made and started preparing to leave that life behind. I was always a good student, so I graduated a year early and made my exit."

"Were you eighteen yet?" Brad asked.

"Not quite, but I would be in a few months."

"Did they allow you to live on your own before you were legal?" Brad asked.

"My social worker knew me pretty well by then and knew I had enough money saved to live on for a while. She also knew that once I was eighteen, I was officially out of the system and she would have no say in what I did, so we kind of compromised. She allowed me to live on my own if I agreed to keep in touch with her and allowed her to visit me until my eighteenth birthday."

"Got it," Brad said.

"So, I found a little apartment and started working on my pilot's license. While I was in pilot's school, I worked at the small regional airport, cleaning, washing, and waxing private planes during the day, and working as a janitor in the airport at night. Once I got my license, I started flying floatplanes for Mountain Air, which is where I met Zander and Jake."

"Did they have the lodge then?" Brad asked.

"Not quite. I flew them back and forth to the lake when they were building the lodge, and when it was finally finished, they offered me a job flying their guests exclusively."

Brad nodded.

"So I rented a plane for the first year, and then, when I'd saved up enough money, finally bought my own, and here we are." Mac sat on the hearth, very relieved to have the story come to an end.

"Mac, I'm sincerely impressed. You overcame some very difficult obstacles. I know a lot of people who have had many more advantages in life and did a lot less with them. You should be very proud of yourself."

"Yeah, well. You do what you have to do to survive."

Brad stood, walked over, and sat next to Mac on the hearth. He put his arm around Mac's shoulder and said, "Your life could have gone in a completely different direction and the outcome could have been a hell of a lot different. You're a hell of a man, Mac."

For a brief second, Mac rested his head on Brad's shoulder. When he realized what he'd done, he quickly stood and said, "Now your turn."

"My story is not nearly as compelling as yours," Brad admitted. "I think it's pretty boring, actually, but with a couple of small similarities."

Mac plopped back onto the couch and said, "I'm all ears."

It was now Brad's turn to pace.

"Okay. I'm an only child and grew up in San Francisco. My mother was a pediatrician, and my father was an attorney. When I was born, my mother became a stay-at-home mom and homeschooled me until the seventh grade. We traveled a good bit, and learning came pretty easy to me. I graduated from Stanford two years early and took a year off to travel alone. That's how I found Hiline Lake. After my year off, I started medical school and specialized in oncology. When I started college, my mother bought a small clinic and went back to work. When I graduated from medical school, she offered me an office in her building, and that's how I started my practice."

Mac smiled and Brad paused and blushed. Suddenly he felt very guilty telling his story. Mac had worked so hard for everything he'd achieved, and here he was, handed everything on a silver platter.

Mac sensed that Brad was struggling with something and he thought he knew what.

"I know what you're thinking Brad," Mac said. "And that's nonsense. We did things differently, all out of our control. We don't pick our parents, and in most cases, they don't pick us. You came from money and I didn't. And you're a doctor and I'm a pilot, not easily comparable," Mac said through a smile. "Tell me more."

"My practice started taking off, and I needed more space. After a year, my mother and I decided to add on to the clinic and that's how I met Jeff. He was the architect we hired to do the plans for the building."

"I was about to ask where Jeff came into the picture." Mac said. "Now it makes sense."

"We instantly fell in love and were almost inseparable," Brad continued. "My parents were always supportive of my lifestyle, and they adored Jeff. And unlike you, Jeff had a family, but they disowned him when they found out he was gay. They never spoke again."

"Are you serious?" Mac asked. "It's stories like this that make me glad I didn't have a family."

"Very serious. In fact, when I called to tell them that he had passed away, they hung up on me."

"Assholes!" Mac said.

"So, like you, my family became his, and life was really good for so many years. One Christmas, my parents took us to Switzerland on a skiing trip, and Jeff and I decided to stay in town and do a little holiday shopping while Mom and Dad skied for the day. There was an avalanche, and they were both killed, along with fifteen other skiers. Needless to say, Jeff and I were devastated. Three years later, Jeff was diagnosed with Stage IV colon cancer, and the rest you know."

They sat in silence for several moments, and Mac finally broke the silence.

"Brad, I don't know what to say. I've never had parents of my own, so I can't say that I know what it must have been like to lose them, but I know what it felt like to lose Lindsey, and that nearly killed me. Then to lose Jeff a few years later… you are one hell of a strong man."

"I don't know about that, but I'm here and you're here, and we survived the challenges we had to face. I guess that makes us both strong men. And Mac, thanks for telling me about your family. I know it couldn't have been easy for you, but you are one hell of a friend, and I love you, man."

Brad and Mac both stood at the same time. Mac took Brad in his arms, and Brad held his embrace.

"Same here," Mac said. "I love you too."

The embrace lasted a little longer than either of them was comfortable with, and Brad broke the hold and stepped back.

"I'm beat, Mac. I think I'll turn in."

Mac said, "I'm not far behind you. If you don't mind, I'll just sit in front of the fire and finish this chapter before I turn in."

"Okay. Night, Mac."

"Sleep tight, Brad, see you in the morning."

"You too."

Brad threw another couple of logs on the fire, put out most of the oil lamps, and went into the bathroom to brush his teeth. When he came out of the bathroom, Mac was lying on the couch with his eyes closed and an open book on his chest. Brad sat on the chair opposite Mac and studied him for a long time. He was very handsome, striking really, and such a great guy. He hadn't realized how attached he'd become to Mac until he was faced with Mac leaving for an unknown amount of time. Mac had come and gone before, but only for a day or two at the most; this time felt different somehow. Neither of them knew when Mac would be able to get back; it all depended on the storm. He was suddenly struck with a feeling of loneliness and longing. Then the realization hit him like a ton of bricks.

Oh my God, do I have feelings for Mac? I can't have feelings for Mac. That's crazy. He's straight, and Jeff's only been dead for six months. Not only did I just lose the love of my life, I think I have feelings for a straight man.

Brad got up from the chair and walked over to his bed. He stood at the foot of the bed and stripped down to his underwear. He pulled back the covers, slipped into bed, and prepared for what he knew would be the worst night's sleep he would have since he moved into the cabin. He propped his pillow against the back of the headboard and watched Mac sleep for the longest time. He saw Mac stretch and get up off the couch. He slid down in his bed and silently watched Mac stoke the fire, turn out the remaining oil lamps, and make his way up to the loft. Obviously Mac thought Brad was sleeping, because when he got to the top of the ladder, he stopped and for several minutes looked intently at Brad lying in bed. Eventually, Mac climbed the rest of the way into the little loft and out of sight. With Mac now in bed, Brad began to toss and turn until he eventually fell into a restless sleep.

MAC slipped into bed with somewhat of a heavy heart. He knew it was best that he was leaving for a while, but it still pained him to desert Brad, especially in the first big storm of the season. But he did have to fly Zander and Jake back to Anchorage, and if they didn't get out before the storm, no one knew when they would get out. His last conscious thought before he fell off to sleep was that he hoped Brad would be okay while he was gone.

Some time later, Mac was awakened by the sound of movement downstairs. *It must be Brad putting more wood on the fire*, he thought. He heard footsteps, then the creak of the ladder, and seconds later he saw Brad's head appear over the floorboards of the loft. Mac sat up in bed and watched as Brad crawled into the tiny loft and sat on the foot of the bed.

"Brad, are you okay?" Mac asked.

"I just needed to be with someone; I hope you don't mind."

Brad looked so sad and lonely that Mac couldn't turn him away.

"Come on," Mac whispered as he pulled back the covers and invited Brad into his bed.

Mac was lying on his side facing Brad as Brad climbed into bed. Brad lay on his back at first, then he turned away from Mac and snuggled his back into him. Mac cautiously put his arm around Brad's waist and held him lightly. A few minutes later, Brad turned over, and Mac looked into Brad's teary eyes. He reached up and lightly brushed the tears off of Brad's cheeks. Brad closed his eyes and put his hand over Mac's and held it against his face.

"I've never felt so alone," Brad whispered.

Mac, no longer in control of his actions, leaned in and softly kissed Brad on the lips.

"Brad, you're not alone. I'm here and will be as long as you need me."

Brad forcefully pressed his lips against Mac's, searching for entry. Mac's mouth opened to the welcomed intrusion, and their tongues danced and explored each other's mouths.

Already, Mac could feel himself getting extremely aroused. He was nervous and confused, but he didn't want to stop. Brad broke the kiss just long enough to pull the sweatshirt over Mac's head, and following Brad's lead, Mac did the same to him.

Again Mac's lips were desperately searching for Brad's. He was so hungry for Brad's taste, it terrified him. Their lips crashed on one another's, and without breaking the kiss, Brad quickly rolled Mac onto his back. Brad lay on top of Mac as their erections grew and he ground his rock-hard dick into Mac's groin. Brad again broke the kiss and slid down under the covers to attend to Mac's growing erection. He pulled Mac's pajama pants off and threw them out of the bed. Mac moaned in ecstasy when Brad nibbled at his engorged dick through the thin cotton of his boxer shorts. Mac ran his fingers through Brad's hair and caressed his neck while Brad explored his body. Mac had no idea it could be like this. He felt so comfortable with Brad. It all seemed so natural and so easy, and he felt both scared and exhilarated at the same time.

Brad worked Mac's boxers down over his hips and slid them off completely. Mac almost came when Brad's tongue licked the crown of his dick. Mac stretched his legs out and squeezed Brad's shoulders hard when Brad took him in completely. Brad slid his mouth back up Mac's long shaft and back down again. Mac had had blow jobs before from women, but not like this. This was incredible. As Brad went down for the third time, Mac saw stars and exploded in Brad's mouth. He felt his orgasm rip through his body like never before. A loud noise made him open his eyes. He sat upright in bed. He was alone. Without thinking, he instinctively called Brad's name.

"Sorry, Mac," Brad said. "It's okay, I dropped a log as I was putting it on the fire. Sorry I woke you."

"Oh, no problem," Mac said shakily, not wanting Brad to hear the panic in his voice.

Horrified, Mac thought, *oh my God, I was dreaming. Not only was I dreaming, I had an orgasm about Brad.* He was too embarrassed to go down to the bathroom, so he took his pajama bottoms and boxers off, cleaned himself with his boxers as best he could, and put his pajama bottoms back on. When he was sure Brad was back in bed, he climbed down the ladder, slipped into the bathroom, and did a better job of cleaning himself.

chapter 15 🛩

THE next morning, Brad lazily opened his bloodshot eyes. He stretched and looked at his watch—*it's a little after ten*. From what he could tell from the streams of light filtering through the window, it looked like a dimly lit morning. *The calm before the storm*, he thought. He stretched again, took a deep breath, and pulled the covers up over his head. He woke up with the same uneasy feeling he'd had when he finally fell asleep. He rolled himself out of bed, put the coffee on, and went to the bathroom to shower and change. When he came out of the bathroom, Mac was still asleep in the loft. He had his first cup of coffee waiting for Mac to wake up. Brad glanced at the clock. *Five after eleven, time to get his ass up*, Brad thought. He climbed the ladder to the loft and saw Mac stretch and pull the pillow over his face.

Mac jumped when Brad smacked the pillow and yelled, "Wake up, before you sleep half the day away."

"What?" Mac mumbled through the pillow. "It's early, you ass."

"Yeah, but today is our last day to make sure everything is secured before the storm, and we have a lot to do," Brad said. "And who are you calling an ass, you dickhead."

Bitter and angry from not sleeping, not to mention his dream, Mac asked, "What's so damn important that it has to be done right this second?"

"For starters, we need to get the new VHF radio hooked up, and get the antenna installed and secured on the roof. I don't want to be stuck out here in a storm with no communication. Next, we need to get the wood box stocked, secure any loose items around the cabin, and make sure this old cabin is buttoned up for a real storm. You won't be here to protect me from Mother Nature's wrath," Brad reminded him.

"Who says you need protecting anyway?" Mac asked.

Brad chuckled. "I'm just teasing, Mac, now get up."

Mac leaned up on his elbows. "For being such an ass, I think you need to bring me a cup of coffee in bed."

"Oh really? If I bring you a cup of coffee, will you get up?"

"Maybe."

"What's gotten into you this morning?" Brad asked. "You're as grumpy as an old spinster."

"Are you always this charming and so full of compliments in the morning?" Mac whined. "First, you call me a dickhead, then an old spinster."

"You called me an ass first, and besides, I said I was just teasing. Don't get your panties in a wad," Brad chuckled.

"Sorry, I didn't sleep very well last night, and to be honest, I'm a little nervous about leaving you to deal with the storm on your own."

"I'm not some mealy mouthed Mellie afraid to be caught in a storm all by my lonesome," Brad said sarcastically.

"Go ahead, make fun, but you're not used to these winter storms up here, Brad. And what in the hell is a mealy mouthed Mellie?" Mac asked.

"Haven't you ever seen the movie *Gone With the Wind*?" Brad asked. "That's what Scarlett O'Hara called Melanie Hamilton when she got engaged to Ashley Wilkes."

"You are so gay," Mac said with a chuckle.

"Look, Mac, seriously, I'll be fine," Brad said over his shoulder as he climbed the ladder to get Mac a cup of coffee. He wobbled back up the ladder using one hand and holding a hot cup of coffee in the other. He sat on the side of Mac's bed and handed him the coffee. "If you can make it back before the worst of it, I know you will. If not, don't worry about it."

As soon as the words left Brad's mouth, he immediately wanted to take them back. He didn't want Mac taking any chances just to get back to him. "I mean, I don't want you risking your life on my account. I'll be fine, really."

"You know I wouldn't take any chances," Mac said. "But if the weather holds out long enough for me to get back, I will."

"I appreciate it, Mac. But again, there's no need."

"We'll see," Mac said.

Brad slapped the bed and said, "Now get up, you lazy breeder."

"Now I'm a lazy breeder?" Mac shouted as he put his coffee on the bedside table and launched himself on top of Brad. Mac pinned him down on the bed, but Brad, being the bigger of the two, quickly flipped Mac over again as they rolled to the floor with a thump. During the roll, Mac landed on top and pinned Brad to the floor.

"Who are you calling a breeder, you pansy?" he shouted. "And besides, I can't have kids, so technically I'm not a breeder," Mac added.

"It's always technicalities with you pilots, isn't it, Mac?"

"If it gets us out of tight spots, why not?"

"Let's see if a technicality can get you out of this spot."

Brad suddenly threw his knees up and rolled to the side, catching Mac off guard. Mac flew off of Brad and hit the floor next to him with a thud. He threw his leg over Mac's chest, and in a flash he was on top again.

Mac felt like Brad was starting to get the best of him, and he wasn't happy about it. He wasn't sure if he was more upset that a gay guy was whipping his ass or that he was causing him to have wet dreams.

"Fine, have it your way. Now get off of me," Mac said through closed teeth.

Brad slipped off of Mac, got to his feet, and offered Mac a hand to help him up. Mac, getting more annoyed by the second, accepted Brad's hand and, catching him off guard this time, pulled Brad back down. Unfortunately, Mac hadn't thought this through, because Brad landed right on top of him. Brad started laughing, which made Mac angrier. Adrenaline kicked in, and he used every bit of force he could gather and rolled Brad over, regaining the top position.

Brad knew Mac was pissed the minute he saw the look on Mac's face. Brad's smile disappeared.

While still on top, straddling Brad at the waist, Mac grabbed two handfuls of Brad's shirt and lifted his back, neck, and head off of the floor. Brad was sure Mac was going to either deck him or slam him back down onto the hardwood floor. He braced himself for the impact, but it didn't come. Instead, everything went silent as Mac brought Brad's face within inches of his own and took his mouth in a demanding kiss.

Brad was very surprised when he felt Mac's tongue press against his lips, seeking entry. He opened to Mac, giving him everything he wanted, as Mac thrust his tongue in, stroking it along the roof of Brad's mouth. Then Brad nibbled along Mac's bottom lip, and Mac moaned and went in deeper. Mac suddenly broke the kiss and raised his head a little. He looked down into Brad's eyes and said, "What are we doing, Brad?"

"I have no idea," Brad replied.

Mac got off of Brad and stood. He offered Brad a hand and helped him to his feet. Brad was still in shock as he watched Mac pull on his pants and climb down the ladder to the kitchen. Brad followed him and put a hand on his shoulder.

"Mac, I'm so sorry. I don't know what came over me."

"What are you sorry for, Brad? I initiated the kiss."

"You kissed me?" Brad asked, surprised.

Mac looked up at Brad and said, "You mean you kissed me?"

"I think we kissed each other," Brad said.

"It appears that way," Mac said. "So now what?"

"Mac, what's going on with you? I've sensed that you've been struggling with something for a while now. I hope I'm not out of line, but the first day we were at the cabin, when I broke down, I thought you almost kissed me. Then I saw your erection when I was bandaging your hand after the burn. Do you think you might be gay?"

"No. I mean, I don't know. I've never been attracted to another guy before." Mac covered his face with his hands. "I don't know what's happening to me," he continued. "When you first showed up at the Lake Hood Air Base, I felt so bad for you. I could see how much pain you were in, and all I wanted to do was help. Then we bought this cabin, and we started spending a lot of time together, and damn if I didn't start experiencing these feelings that I can't explain.

"At first I told myself that the feelings were just because I'd been where you are and I felt so damn bad for you. But the more time we spent together, the stronger the attraction got, and, Brad, it scares the hell out of me. I've never had feelings for another man. I mean, I played around a little in high school, but it was all physical and just fooling around. Not to mention the fact that you lost Jeff only six months ago. You're not in any position to get involved with anyone, especially a man with identity issues."

"Mac, you're right," Brad replied. "I don't know what I'm ready for right now, but to be totally honest, last night I realized that I was developing feelings for you as well. I've been getting so attached to you over the last few months, and I thought it was normal after what I—we'd—been through, but when you fell asleep last night on the couch, I sat there and watched you sleep for the longest time. The cabin was quiet, and it was me, you, and the fire. I thought about my life without you in it, and suddenly I felt as lonely as the day Jeff died. The feelings came at me really hard. I don't know what they are, and I don't know if I'm quite ready to pursue them, but I told myself that even if I wanted to pursue them, you were straight, or at least I thought you were. So I needed to put them out of my head."

Mac looked up at Brad with teary eyes. "So what do we do now?"

"I don't know, Mac, but just so we're clear, I wanted to kiss you as much as you say you wanted to kiss me."

Mac smiled a little at that admission. He looked out the window and thought about the approaching storm. "I think we better table this for now," he said. "We both have a lot to think about and a lot to do today. Let's take the day, get our chores done, and we'll talk about this later."

"Good idea," Brad said.

chapter 16

THEY spent most of the morning in silence and pretty much stuck to the chores at hand until lunch. They took a break and ate a sandwich, and Mac was the first to speak. "So what do you think the ID for the cabin should be?" he asked, referring to the new VHF radio.

"Wow, I hadn't thought about that," Brad said.

"Well, when you first showed this place to me, you called it Tumbling Downs," Mac said. "How about that?"

"How would that sound over a radio?" Brad asked.

"Let's see," Mac said. "'November 4649 Delta calling Tumbling Downs'."

"What do you think?" Brad asked. "Not so good, huh?"

"Not so much," Mac said.

"Any other suggestions?" Brad asked.

"Let me noodle on it a second." A thought popped into his mind. "Okay, how about this? Since I'm a pilot and you're an excellent wingman, and we live in this mansion, how about Wing Mansion?" Mac asked.

"Look at you," Brad said. "I like it. Wing Mansion it is."

Things seemed to lighten up just a little, and they went back to work. By five thirty, they were about done. Everything was secured, the wood box was filled to capacity, the new radio was set up, the shutters were closed and secured, and the large solar panels and new VHF antenna on the roof were reinforced and protected.

In the afternoon hours, not ready to be finished, Mac was stacking another cord of wood on the back porch, in case the storm went longer than expected and Brad got really snowed in. Brad was now happy for the solitude, but knew Mac was trying his best to take care of him, and that both scared and comforted him at the same time. He sat on the front porch and looked up at the sky. The clouds were starting to roll in, and the sky had taken on a gray hue that hinted of the coming snowstorm. He looked out over the mountains. All the thoughts that had rolled around his head during the day came flooding to the surface. *What am I doing? Jeff died six months ago. How can I be feeling something for someone else, especially a straight man? A straight man who may not be so straight... I'm not ready for this. I need time to think this through. He's a great guy, and obviously he's attracted to me, which is strange in itself, but what do I do? I don't want to hurt his feelings, but I need more time. I hope he'll understand.*

Brad was startled out of his thoughts when Mac sat next to him on the porch.

"I think you're ready for the blow," Mac said.

"Why McGovern Cleary, how dare you be so blunt," Brad said in a Southern voice, knowing well and good that Mac was referring to the coming storm.

"Oh, that's very funny," Mac shot back.

"I'm just kidding," Brad said. "I had to say something to break the tension around here. It's so thick, I could have cut it with the chain saw."

"I know and I'm sorry; I just had to work this out in my head."

"Yeah, me too, but I hope you had better luck than I did."

"Not so much," Mac responded.

Brad frowned. "What say we get showered, have some wine, watch the sun go down, and talk this through? Real open and honest talk, no beating around the bush, just put all our cards on the table?"

"I think that's a great idea," Mac said.

"Okay, I'll go shower while you open the wine," said Brad.

"Deal."

When Brad was showered and changed, he came out of the bathroom. Mac was in the kitchen preparing a plate of cheese, fresh fruit, and crackers. Brad stood next to him and poured each of them a glass of wine from the opened bottle.

Mac noticed how clean and woodsy Brad smelled, and he savored the fresh scent.

While Mac showered, Brad retrieved two rocking chairs from the storage shed and put them in their normal spot on the porch. He figured he would just bring them into the cabin when they went to bed, and they could stay there until the storm passed.

Ten minutes later, Mac was opening the screen door with his wet hair slicked back and a shy smile on his face.

He sat next to Brad and picked up his glass of wine.

"So, what's new?"

They both laughed and seemed to relax a little.

They said each other's name at the same time and laughed again.

"Okay, you go first," Brad said.

Looking ahead at the horizon over the mountain tops, Mac opened his mouth to speak, and then he closed it. He looked at Brad, and then looked back at the horizon again.

Brad smiled, "You want me to go first?" he asked.

"Nope, I can do this. I'm a big boy. But please let me get through this before you say anything."

Brad nodded in agreement.

"Okay," Mac said as he turned and looked directly into Brad's beautiful green eyes. "I don't know what this is. I've never been attracted to a man before, and I don't know how to deal with it. It scares the shit out of me. As I mentioned earlier, at first I thought the attraction was just because we shared a bond over losing our partners. I mean, I really felt for you. I knew exactly what you were going through, and I wanted so much to help you. Then the feelings kept getting stronger, and the more I tried to push them back, the stronger they became. I'm not gay, Brad," Mac continued.

Brad looked sadly into Mac's eyes and listened intently. He could see Mac was really struggling.

"At least I didn't think I was gay. Lindsey was the love of my life, and from the day I married her, I've never even looked at another woman, not to mention a man, for God's sake, so why now?

"I've felt more alive in the last four months than I have in the last five years. I didn't realize how lonely I was until I started spending time with you. You and this cabin have given me something to live for. Since Lindsey died, I've gone through life on autopilot, so to speak—I raised Zoe-Grace, and I thought I was doing okay, but I wasn't really living. I was just going through the motions. But, Brad, I'm not gay.

"What would Lindsey think, and oh God, Zoe and Jack? They're the only family I have besides my half sister. How would I tell them? I don't even know what to do with a man, how to act, how to feel. Brad, I'm very attracted to you, and I think I have real feelings for you, but I don't know how to act on them, or if I even *want* to act on them. Does that make me a coward?"

Brad opened his mouth to speak.

"No, don't answer that. I'm not through yet."

Brad closed his mouth and took a deep breath.

"I love it here," Mac continued. "If I chose not to act on this thing between us, will it ruin our friendship? Can I still come up here? Hell, I don't even know if you want me to act on this. Brad, help me out here."

"Can I speak now?" Brad said with a smile.

"God yes," Mac said. "Please, I'm burying myself faster than an undertaker."

"For starters, I don't know what this thing is either. I am gay and have been all my life, so I don't know any other way of life. That part is a no-brainer for me. I thought that my attachment to you was just gratitude for helping me get through Jeff's death. Then the stronger I became, the stronger the attachment became. I don't know what these feelings are, and whatever they are, I know I denied them at first and tried to subconsciously push them away. But I think, at some point, I would like to see where they go, when I'm ready—and if you even want to. I'm not ready to let Jeff go, and I know that's not really fair to you, but I need to sort this through, just as you do. Whatever we decide, this can't ruin our friendship. I need you and…." Looking around and gesturing to the surroundings, he finished, "I need this."

Brad put his hand out, open palm up, and looked at Mac. Mac slowly and reluctantly slipped his hand into Brad's and entwined their fingers. They stayed that way in silence, sipping their wine and watching the sun dip behind the mountaintops like they had done so many times before. Only this time, it was different, very different.

Mac broke the silence. "Well, I think everything's on the table," he said. "Tomorrow morning, I'll be out of here for a while, and I think the time away will be good for both of us."

Mac started to say something else, then stopped.

"What is it, Mac?" Brad asked.

Mac opened his mouth to speak again, but only hesitated this time before he spoke. "This might sound stupid, but tonight, let's just enjoy each other's company and do what feels right. No labels, no questions, and no analyzing. I want to see what it feels like to just be with you, just hang out as if we were a couple, with no anticipation of what will or will not be."

"It doesn't sound stupid at all, Mac. I think I'd like that."

When they could no longer see the glow of the sun behind the mountain and the chill had started to set in, still hand in hand, Mac stood. He looked down at Brad. "How about we move inside? It's getting a little chilly."

"Sure," Brad said.

Before Brad could stand, Mac pulled him out of his chair into a standing position and put his arms around Brad's waist. He moved hesitantly, but buried his head in Brad's neck and inhaled Brad's scent. It felt strange, but comfortable at the same time. He exhaled and gently kissed Brad's neck. He held his lips there, savoring the taste of Brad's skin.

Brad slowly wrapped his arms around Mac's neck, closed his eyes, and leaned into the embrace. He thought how good it felt to be held by a pair of strong arms again. He struggled to push thoughts of Jeff out of his mind and tried to focus on the here and now.

They stayed that way for a few minutes, experiencing the new sensations and simply enjoying the moment.

Mac stepped away from the embrace first. He handed Brad the wine bottle and grabbed the plate of cheese and fruit and the wine glasses. He took Brad's hand and led him inside. Mac poured them each another glass, and while he started a fire, Brad went about lighting the oil lamps. When all was done, they sat on the couch, but this time next to each other.

"A penny for your thoughts?" Brad asked.

"Well, I was just thinking that we've done this drill so many times since we bought this little cabin. I make the fire, you light the lamps... but somehow it feels different tonight."

"Different how?" Brad asked.

"I'm not sure, just different."

"I think I know what you mean, Mac, but I can't quite put my finger on it either."

"Thank goodness," Mac said. "At least I'm not the only crazy one."

"I think we've already established that." Brad chuckled.

"So what now?" Mac asked.

"What are you looking at me for?" Brad said guardedly. "This is just as weird for me as it is for you."

"Yeah, but you've done this before," Mac said.

"Done what?" Brad asked.

"You know, been with a guy."

"Are you serious?" Brad said with a hint of sarcasm.

"Well, kind of," Mac said.

"Look, Mac, I don't know what you think happens with two guys, but it's pretty much the same thing as a guy and a girl. And to be honest, I haven't had that much experience. Jeff was only the second guy I ever dated. So I'm just as nervous as you are."

"Then we're pretty much screwed," Mac chuckled.

"Isn't that usually the end result anyway?" Brad asked.

"Pretty much," Mac responded, and they both laughed.

Mac took a sip of his wine and got up to stoke the fire.

"I guess we should start to think about dinner," Brad said.

"Yeah, I'm getting pretty hungry. How about I throw a couple of steaks on the fire, and you put two potatoes in the microwave," Mac said. "That shouldn't take us too long, and then we can relax for the rest of the evening."

"Great idea," Brad said.

While Mac prepared the steaks, Brad stabbed the potatoes with a fork, wrapped them in damp paper towels and popped them in the microwave. Mac skewered the steaks and placed them on the rack in the fireplace. They had both mentally thanked Seth over the last few months for installing the battery-operated rotisserie and grilling rack in the fireplace several years back. It really made grilling easy.

In about fifteen minutes, they were eating like kings and enjoying a second bottle of wine. When they were through, Brad headed to the kitchen to start the cleanup process. Mac joined him, and Brad couldn't help but notice how their hands and shoulders brushed against each other's a little more than usual. But he liked it.

When they were finished, Mac threw himself on one end of the couch with his legs spread over the length of the couch. When Brad joined him, Mac pulled up his knees as an invitation, and Brad sat on the other end of the couch. Mac stretched his legs out again and lay his feet on Brad's lap.

Brad removed both of Mac's slippers and started to rub Mac's feet. Mac leaned his head back on the arm of the couch and closed his eyes.

Mac opened one eye and said, "That feels really good."

"Just lay back and relax. I got pretty good at this when Jeff was sick, it made...." He stopped and said, "Never mind. Relax and enjoy."

Mac closed his eyes again and did what he was told. Brad again tried to put Jeff out of his mind. This would take some getting used to. He'd done nothing but think about Jeff for the last six months, and now he was trying to block him out of his mind for one night.

Brad watched the look of comfort on Mac's face. Mac seemed really relaxed, and Brad was glad he could do that for him. Mac had done so much for him, and he couldn't think of a way to pay him back. Maybe this was a little way he could show Mac how much he appreciated him. When Brad finished one foot, he massaged the second foot until Mac was purring like a kitten. He slipped out from under Mac's legs and headed for the kitchen to refill their wine glasses, and as he passed Mac's head, Mac grabbed his legs.

"Where do you think you're going?"

"Shhhh... to get more wine," he whispered. "Go back to sleep."

Mac pulled on Brad's legs, and Brad landed on top of him.

"Whoa, flyboy," Brad said.

"What makes you think I was asleep?" Mac asked.

"The fact that you were snoring, to start with," Brad said.

"Was not," Mac snapped back.

"Was too," Brad said.

Mac smiled, raised his head, and plastered a quick kiss on Brad's lips. Brad kissed him back as an invitation, and Mac went in deeper for another. Brad opened his mouth at Mac's silent request, and they both gave way to the intimacy of it all. Brad was the first to pull away this time. Mac looked disappointed, but he held Brad's gaze.

"This all feels so natural and easy," Brad said. "Being with you like this. I never imagined ever being with anyone else, especially you."

"Thanks a lot," Mac said.

"No, I didn't mean it like that, you know what I mean," Brad responded.

"Brad, you can see that I'm struggling with this too, but at the same time, it does feel really good."

"Mac, this isn't an easy life. Although things have gotten so much better, there are still a lot of prejudices out there. Sure, we're able to marry in a few states, but at what cost?"

Mac tilted his head and looked at Brad. "Brad, I still don't think that I'm gay. If I were to leave this cabin tomorrow and never see you again, I don't think I would ever look at another guy. Does that sound weird?"

"Not really," Brad said. "I have this theory about sexuality. Do you want to hear it?"

"Sure," Mac said as he nudged his way over on the couch and Brad slid in between him and the back of the couch. "Okay, shoot," Mac said.

"I believe that, in general, people are born sexual. I think that if society didn't tell us who it was and wasn't okay to be with, and everyone could be with whomever they chose without persecution, I believe that there would be many more same-sex couples. People are drawn to one another many times in life for many reasons. But if it were as 'normal and accepted' to be in a same-sex relationship as it were to be in an opposite-sex relationship, then those same people would probably find their way to each other romantically. If people had the right to choose a same-sex partner without prejudice, I think they would," Brad continued.

"So you're right, you could leave here tomorrow and never ever look at another guy, because society says it's not okay to do so. Remember, we didn't start out our friendship with the hopes of any type of romantic relationship. It just sort of happened. We had something in common in the beginning that bonded us together, and then we got to know one another on a one-on-one basis and found out that we enjoyed each other's company, and we were open enough to see that there might be something between us."

"Wow, that's some theory," Mac said.

"Do you disagree?" Brad asked.

"No, I don't think so. I just never heard it put that way, and it does make a lot of sense. I mean, in my opinion, hatred and prejudice is something we're taught, not something we're born with. It's like, when we're young kids, we don't see other kids as different because of the color of their skin or the size of their body, but then we grow and all hell breaks loose."

"Exactly," Brad said. "But, Mac, also remember being gay or together up here when it's just the two of us is very different from the real world. I've never hidden who I am, and I would never do that. We are so far away from that ever being an issue, but it's something you have to think about while you're away. I believe there is something between us that we can explore if and when we want to—when I'm ready and if you're ever ready—but the decision to be with another man is not something to be taken lightly. You can't go back. I've never wanted to go back because I've always known who I am, but you haven't been so fortunate."

Mac jabbed him in the gut, and he laughed. "I'm just kidding, but you know what I'm trying to say."

"Yeah, I get it," Mac said. "But, Brad, please understand something. I don't take relationships lightly. When I make a commitment, I keep it, and if I were to ever make a commitment to you or anyone else, I would honor it until the end. When I love, I love all the way. There's no halfway, it's all or nothing."

"I'll remember that," Brad said.

"Now, let's get some sleep," Mac said. "I have to get up very early to beat this storm."

"Mac?"

"Yeah?"

"Would you like to bunk in with me—I mean, just sleep with me?"

Mac hesitated and Brad said, "Never mind, that's probably a bad idea."

"Yeah," Mac said.

"Yeah what?"

"Yeah, I would like to sleep with you."

They got up and each went through their normal routine to get ready for bed.

When they were through, they both walked to Brad's bed and stopped at the foot. Mac reached out and took Brad into an embrace and gently kissed him on the cheek. They stripped down to their boxers and T-shirts and climbed into bed. Mac thought about how Brad slid in and snuggled his back into him, as Brad had done in his dream. Mac put his arm around Brad's waist and pulled him close.

"This is nice," Mac said.

"It is," Brad responded.

Mac again buried his nose in Brad's neck and inhaled Brad's scent. He gently kissed him on the neck and said, "Good night, Brad."

"Night, Mac."

Mac closed his eyes and thought about the road he was heading down, and tried to separate his heart from his head, but it didn't work. If he were to get involved with Brad, he had to know what he was getting into. Brad didn't deserve to have half of him, and he certainly didn't deserve to be hurt after working so hard to get over Jeff's death. *I have to be certain*, was his last thought as he fell off to a comfortable sleep with Brad wrapped in his arms.

Brad lay awake, thinking about the man in his bed. *When had this happened?* When had he gone from losing Jeff to having feelings for Mac? It all seemed so odd, but he did think he had strong feelings for Mac. It was asking an awful lot of Mac to commit to a life with him, if it came to that. He needed more time to think about all of this. *What would Jeff think?* Neither of them had gone out looking for this, it just happened—surely Jeff knew that. *I have to be certain*, was his last thought as he fell off to a comfortable sleep, wrapped in Mac's protective arms.

chapter 17

BRAD woke up in the same position in which he had fallen asleep. He instinctively glanced at the clock—*Six thirty-two. Damn, why did I sleep so late?* He glanced at the window, which was part of his wake-up routine, and remembered it would still be dark outside. Then he remembered he and Mac had closed and secured all the shutters yesterday. Mac! He suddenly remembered that he'd gone to sleep in Mac's arms. Unconsciously, he reached behind him for the comfort he'd experienced during the night, but the bed was empty.

He sat up and looked around the cabin. Mac was gone. "Mac?" he called. No answer. He got up and checked the bathroom; it was empty. He climbed the ladder to the loft. Mac's bed was as it had been the day before. He opened the front door and immediately felt a chill. Mac wasn't here. Disappointment overtook him as he closed the door. He walked to the kitchen to start the coffee when he saw the note on the kitchen table.

> Good morning sleepyhead,
>
> I hope you don't mind that I snuck out, but you were sleeping so soundly, I didn't want to wake you. I left around five thirty so I could make it to the lake, get the plane ready for an early flight, and get out before the storm hits. Please believe me when I say that my leaving without saying good-bye had nothing to do with you, our conversation, or our night together. I just thought it might be easier on both of us to not have to say good-

bye right now. We both have so much to
think about, and I know neither of us will
take any of this lightly, but I do know that
whatever happens, I never want to lose your
friendship. I'll always hold you in the highest
regard, and I'll always be here for you, if and
when you need me. I also know that the loss
of Jeff is still fresh in your heart and mind,
and I don't even know how to begin to
compete with his memory. So basically, I can
decide whatever I decide, but this all depends
on you and if you'll ever be ready to open
your heart to anyone else.

I'm as confused as I've ever been in my
life, and I don't know what to think of all
these emotions and, more importantly, how
to sort through them. Lindsey always said
that "the heart wants what it wants" even if
it's a difficult situation. And for the first
time, I really see what she meant.

I know you're nervous about being here
all alone for the first storm of the season, but
I know you'll be okay. Even though we both
need a little time away, if I can possibly get
back before the storm hits, I will. Take care
and if you need me, use the VHF radio, and I
will always be here.

Mac

He put the letter down and looked around the little cabin.
Between the darkness of the windows and the silence and the chill
of the early morning, he felt very lonely.

He walked to the table where the VHF radio was and picked
up the handset. He raised it to his mouth and almost started to speak.
He put it back down and stepped away.

He needs time, he thought. *He said that in his letter. But I want to make sure he's okay. Fuck time. I need to talk to him.*

He stepped up to the radio, picked up the handset, and pressed the button. "November 4649 Delta, this is Wing Mansion. Over."

He waited for a few seconds and heard nothing.

"November 4649 Delta, this is Wing Mansion, do you copy?"

He waited again.

Just when he was about to repeat the call again, he heard, "Wing Mansion, this is November 4649 Delta, I hear you loud and clear. Wing Mansion, switch to channel one eight. Over," he heard Mac's voice say.

"Wing Mansion switching to channel one eight," Brad repeated.

Brad turned the dial up two notches to channel one eight and said, "Wing Mansion standing by on channel one eight."

"Good morning sleepyhead. Over," Mac said.

"Mac, are you okay? Over." Brad asked.

"I'm fine. Did you get my note? Over."

"Mac, thank you for taking the time to write it; it was very thoughtful. Over."

"That's me, thoughtful Mac. Over."

Mac was sounding a little strange. Then Brad remembered Zander and Jake were with him, and he was sure they could hear everything Mac was saying.

"Mac, I know Zander and Jake can hear what you're saying, but can they hear me? Over."

"That's a negative. Over," Mac responded.

"Oh good, I'm not ready to start explaining all of this to them. Over."

"That's affirmative. Over," Mac said.

"What's your ETA? Over," Brad asked.

"About zero eight hundred hours. Over," Mac said.

Brad remembered military time, and he thought that meant eight am. "Okay, safe flight and give my best to Zander and Jake, and tell them to enjoy their vacation and not to worry about the lodge. I'll check on it every couple of days. Over."

"I'll pass that along. Over," Mac responded.

"Mac, will you make it back up before the storm? Over."

"I'll do my best, but if I don't, you'll be fine. I'll be in touch. Over."

"I'll look forward to it. Oh, and Mac, please be careful. I don't want to lose you. Over."

"Will do. Over."

Brad ended the conversation by saying, "You do that." He added, "Wing Mansion over and out, switching back to channel one six."

The last thing Brad heard Mac say was, "November 4649 Delta standing by on channel one six."

chapter 18 ✈

BRAD put the handset down, but left the radio on, hoping to hear Mac's request to land at Lake Hood. He walked back to his bed and climbed in on the side that Mac had slept on. The sheets and pillow still smelled like Mac. He took a deep breath and inhaled Mac's scent. He wrapped himself in the sheets and buried his head in Mac's pillow and stayed there, breathing him in. For the first time in a very long time, he felt a stirring in his groin. Brad realized that he was experiencing his first erection since Jeff went into the hospital. All at once he was shocked and a little embarrassed. He slid his hand down his boxer shorts and caressed his erection. It had been so long since he'd even thought of sex. Even last night, lying next to Mac, he had been content just to sleep in Mac's arms—sex never entered his mind.

Not that he wasn't attracted to Mac; he was a gorgeous man. But now, he was alone in his cabin, Mac was in Anchorage, and he was a healthy male, the hell with it. Without realizing he was already stroking his erection, he rubbed his fingers around the crown of his dick, across his slit, and down the length and back up. *This feels damn good*, he thought. He wished he had some lube, but he just wasn't prepared.

Although he started off thinking about Mac, in his fantasy he saw Jeff jacking him off and staring at him with such desire. He smiled at the thought, then Jeff's face faded away and slowly turned into Mac's, and he was suddenly filled with mixed emotions. It had always been Jeff, and now it was Mac and Jeff. He saw Mac's face so clearly. His beautiful blue eyes were looking deeply into his. But now Jeff was standing over Mac's shoulder, watching Mac stroke his engorged dick. Jeff was smiling and rubbing Mac's shoulders as if in approval. Even though he and Jeff had never had a three-way, suddenly the thought was about to send him over the top. Another couple of strokes and he felt his balls tightening up. He pulled the sheet down and lifted his T-shirt as the first spurt almost reached his chest. He pumped his dick harder and harder, and the second and third spurts landed on his tight stomach. He lay there, somewhere between feeling guilty and confused and very satisfied.

Mac's voice, filled with static, broke the silence.

"This is November 4649 Delta calling Lake Hood air traffic control tower, do you copy?"

"November 4649 Delta, this is the tower at Lake Hood, I read you loud and clear and have you on radar. Welcome back, Mac. Hold your current heading, I have a couple guys ahead of you. Over."

Brad sat up in bed and listened.

"Roger that," he heard Mac say. "November 4649 Delta standing by on channel one six."

Brad thought how weird it felt, listening to Mac on the radio when he had just fantasized about him in the very spot Mac had slept the night before. Before he could elaborate his thoughts, he heard, "November 4649 Delta, this is the Lake Hood tower, do you copy?"

"November 4649 Delta, I read you loud and clear," he heard Mac say.

"November 4649 Delta, switch to channel three eight. Over."

"November 4649 Delta switching to channel three eight."

Brad wiped his stomach with his T-shirt and ran over to the radio and changed the channel to three eight.

He heard, through more static this time, Mac saying, "November 4649 Delta standing by on three eight. Over."

"Hey, Mac, this is Dan, how's it going, man? Over," Brad heard a strange voice say.

"Hey, Dan, going great. When are we going to have that beer we've been talking about? Over," Mac said.

"Just say the word, Mac. I've got someone I want you to meet. Over," the new voice said.

"Oh shit," Brad said under his breath.

"Oh really. Over," Mac replied.

"Yeah, my wife's girlfriend just moved back to Anchorage after a nasty divorce, and she is really something. Over."

He's trying to set Mac up on a date with a divorcée, Brad thought.

"Thanks for thinking about me, Dan, but I'm kinda seeing someone. Over," Mac said.

"Holy shit," Brad said again under his breath. *Did he just say he was seeing someone? Is he talking about me?*

"Anyone I know? Over," Dan asked.

"No, not really, it's in the early stages, but I'm very interested. Over."

"Let me know if things change. Over," Dan said.

"Will do. How about getting me on the ground? Over."

"Sure thing, Mac. Change your heading to five eight nine, and you're cleared to land. Over."

"November 4649 Delta changing heading to five eight nine. Over."

Brad stood in front of the radio with his mouth opened wide. *We're dating?*

A smile came over his face while he stood in a soiled T-shirt and boxers staring at a VHF radio.

Once on the ground, he heard Mac switch back to channel sixteen, and he did the same. He felt relieved that Mac was safe on the ground and possibly in enough time to get back before the storm.

He turned on the weather radio for an update and walked to the kitchen to start some long overdue coffee.

The weather forecast said the storm would be approaching the mountain range just before noon, which—if correct—gave Mac enough time to get back before the worst hit. He crossed his fingers that Mac would try to get back, but he couldn't push. He would be okay alone, but would prefer Mac here with him.

How strange, he thought as he poured his cup of coffee. *Just four months ago, I was prepared to spend the rest of my life up here in solitude, and now I can't even spend a few days without Mac. God, have I gotten that attached to him?* He knew the answer was yes, but he also knew that he was setting himself up for the possibility of a big fall. *Mac's not even sure he wants to pursue a relationship with me. What if I open up to him, and he decides he just can't do it? What then? Can I take another loss?*

He frowned slightly when he realized there were no easy answers. They were both taking a huge risk. *Mac's not sure if I am ready to move on with him, and I'm not sure Mac can or will move on with me. Something or someone has gotta give.*

Brad finished his coffee, took a quick shower, dressed, and poured himself another cup of coffee. It was a little after eight, and by God, if he was going to get snowed in, alone or otherwise, he was going to enjoy the morning.

chapter 19 ✈

AS PLANNED, Mac touched down with Zander and Jake just after eight. He taxied over to his normal dock on the lake, shut down the engine, and helped the guys get their luggage off the plane. Mac kept the conversation light, because he knew they'd heard not only the one-sided conversation between him and Brad, but also the conversation between him and Dan, the air traffic controller. He'd glanced back over his shoulder during the conversation with Dan, and both Zander and Jake were looking at each other with confused expressions on their faces.

Why did I say I was dating someone? They know I've been spending all of my time at the cabin, he thought as he unloaded the luggage. *I don't want to get into this with them, not now. And besides, it could be nothing. What am I going to tell them? I might be gay. I might be in love with Brad. Brad may not even want me. Oh man.*

Luckily, neither of the guys said anything about the radio conversations as Mac helped them carry their bags to their truck. When they got to the parking lot, they exchanged hugs, and Mac wished them well and agreed to pick them up in a week.

"Have a safe flight back to the lake," Zander said. "But don't take any chances."

Surprised, Mac said, "What? I'm not even sure I'm going back up before the storm."

"Sure you are," Jake said. "Just be careful."

The guys hopped into their truck and waved as they drove away.

What did they pick up on? he thought as he walked back to the terminal.

Mac went straight to his kiosk and turned on his weather radio. According to the latest update, the storm wasn't going to come over the mountain range until around noon or so. That gave him plenty of time to refuel and head back up. If all went well, he could be back by eleven.

He called the fuel truck to meet him at his dock, and while he was waiting, he called Zoe-Grace. He got her voicemail and left a message. "Hey, honey, it's Dad. Just checking in and so looking forward to seeing you at Christmas. I'm headed back up to the lake, so I won't be able to call you back, but if your plans change, just leave me a voicemail and I'll get it next time I get cell service. I love you. Bye."

Keeping his promise to Jack to do a better job at keeping in touch, he dialed Jack's number and waited for the ring.

"Hello," Jack said.

"Hey, Jack, it's Mac."

"Hey, man, what's up?"

"Not a hell of a lot. I just did a touch-and-go from the lake to bring Zander and Jake down for their vacation, and I'm fueling up and headed right back up."

"You do know a storm's on its way, don't you?" Jack asked.

"Yes, smart-ass, I know a storm's on its way."

"Do you think you have enough time to make it back up?" Jack asked.

"Oh yeah, plenty," Mac responded.

"Hey, Mac, when am I going to get to come up and see that cabin of yours?"

"What's your schedule next week?" Mac asked.

"Not much. The boat will be out of the water for some much needed maintenance, and I was planning to just hang around."

"I tell you what, I have to fly back to pick up Zander and Jake a week from today. Why don't you fly back up with us and stay the week or however long you want?"

"That sounds perfect," Jack said.

"It's a plan then. Be here and ready to fly by nine thirty, and we'll have a little adventure."

"Sounds great. Are you sure it's okay with Brad?" Jack asked.

"I'm sure it'll be fine, but I'll let you know if anything changes. If you don't hear from me, then everything's a go," Mac replied.

"Good deal, Mac, and have a safe flight."

"Will do. Bye, Jack, see you next week."

"Bye Mac."

FOR once, all went as planned, and by nine thirty, he was requesting takeoff. Once he was at cruising altitude, he sat back and enjoyed the ride.

His mind started to wander. *I guess I really do want to try this thing with Brad. But when did I decide that? One minute I was unsure, the next I was telling Dan that I was seeing someone. Boy, that really says it all. I've never been gay before. I wonder what it's like.*

Mac, just relax and take it one step at a time. Brad would never push you to do anything you weren't ready for. But what about Brad? I sure hope he feels the same way. I can't push him, he's been through so much. I've got to be patient.

BRAD opened the front door and was blinded by the bright morning. The clouds were moving in and the temperature had dropped considerably, but the sun was peeking out through a few holes in the clouds, and compared to the cool darkness of the cabin, he felt a little more energized.

While he sipped his coffee, he took a stroll around the cabin again, making sure everything was secure. Once he was satisfied everything was done, he poured himself yet another cup and sat on one of the rocking chairs on the porch. He still couldn't believe what he'd heard on the radio. He smiled and looked out over the lake, willing Mac's little plane to appear. He kept an eye out for Mac for another thirty minutes or so and then figured he just couldn't make it back. The sky was getting that gray look it gets just before it dumps tons of snow on you, so he figured it was time to go inside. He carried both chairs from the porch and placed them just inside the cabin door and then closed the front door. He was loading a few logs in the fireplace and preparing to light a fire to get ready for the dropping temps when he heard Mac's familiar voice.

"November 4649 Delta calling Wing Mansion, Wing Mansion do you copy? Over."

Brad dropped the logs and ran to the radio.

"This is Wing Mansion. Mac, are you okay? Over," Brad asked.

"Wing Mansion, can you switch to channel one eight? Over."

Brad repeated, "Wing Mansion switching to channel one eight. This is Wing Mansion on channel one eight."

Brad held his breath, waiting to see if Mac was okay or not.

He sighed when he heard Mac say, "Hey, Bradford, top of the morning to you. Over."

"Hey, flyboy, great to hear your voice. Where are you? Over."

"About twenty minutes from the lake."

Yeah! Brad said to himself.

"How's it looking at the lake? Over."

"Pretty gloomy," Brad said. "The clouds are moving in fast, and the temperature is dropping. Can you push it a little and get here any quicker? Over."

"I'll see what I can do. Over."

"Okay, I'll start hiking down to the dock and meet you halfway."

"Roger that."

"Oh, and Mac, thank you for coming back up. I'm so glad you're almost here. Over."

"Me too. See you soon. Over."

"Roger that and be careful. Over."

"This is November 4649 Delta switching to channel one six."

"Wing Mansion switching back to channel one six."

Brad could hardly contain himself. He grabbed his coat and tore out of the front door.

Mac touched down on the lake five minutes ahead of schedule. He taxied straight over to the beach instead of the dock. A couple of years back, Zander and Jake had helped him sink stakes to which he could secure cables to keep the plane tied down in the event of high winds. To secure the wings, one end of the cable was hooked to the stake and the other to a grommet on the tip of each wing, while the other two stakes secured the aft by a cable looped over the tail.

With the plane secured, he grabbed his backpack and started toward the cabin. He looked up at the sky. *Brad was right, the clouds are moving in fast*, he thought. *I better get a move on.* He zipped up his jacket, threw his backpack over his shoulder, and started on his way.

He felt unusually light on his feet and had a real bounce in his step. About twenty minutes into his walk, he realized he was singing. *Damn, I must have it bad. I don't sing*, he thought. He smiled to himself and kept walking and… singing. He'd been on the trail a little while when he rounded a bend and something slammed into him and knocked him on his ass.

BRAD was about ten minutes into his hike down to the lake when he heard the hum of Mac's plane above the treetops. Through a clearing, he caught a glimpse of the little plane as it safely touched down on the lake. He said a silent thank you and picked up his pace. In another thirty minutes, he heard Mac's voice before he saw him. Mac was singing: "Oh what a beautiful morning, oh what a beautiful day! I've got a wonderful feeling, everything's going my way." He made a mental note to tease Mac relentlessly about his lack of ability to carry a tune in a bucket. He laughed out loud and started running down the trail. When he rounded a bend in the trail, he ran smack into Mac, and they bounced off of one another, and both landed on their asses.

Stunned, Mac said, "What the…?" When he realized it was Brad who'd knocked him down, he shook his head and smiled. "Now that's some welcome, Bradford," he said as his smile broadened.

"Sorry," Brad said.

"Don't be." Mac chuckled. "No one's ever this happy to see me."

"What makes you think I'm happy to see you?" Brad asked.

Mac looked down and said, "Well… I just thought… sorry, I didn't mean to…."

Before Mac could finish his sentence, Brad pounced on him, threw his arms around Mac's neck, and planted a big kiss on his lips.

"I'm real happy to see you," Brad confessed.

"Now, that's more like it," Mac said. "But are you happy because I'm back or because you don't have to be alone for the storm?"

"What do you think?" Brad said with a slight pout.

Brad stood and offered a hand to Mac. Mac accepted it, and Brad pulled him to his feet.

They started back to the cabin, and Mac reached out and took Brad's hand. They walked hand in hand in silence for a portion of the walk back to the cabin, just happy to be together.

They both stopped and looked up as the first snowflakes of the winter started to float to the ground. Mac suggested they step up their pace, and it was a good thing because they just made it back to the cabin before the winds picked up and the snow really started to fall. They stood hand in hand on the porch for a few minutes as they watched the first blizzard of the winter season move in.

chapter 20

NOW that he was back and Brad wouldn't be alone, Mac opened a couple of the shutters to the windows that were protected under the porch, so they could watch the storm from inside. He figured if the winds got too strong, he could close them without any problems.

When the fire was blazing and a few oil lamps were lit, they both changed into flannel pajama bottoms, long-sleeved T-shirts, and heavy wool socks.

Mac poured them each a brandy, and they sat side by side on the couch, positioned so that they could both look out of the windows and watch the snow falling.

"Mac, I really appreciate you coming back up. I could have certainly made it alone, but I'm so glad you're here."

"I'm glad I came back too. It's really strange… we were only apart for a few hours, but I felt like I'd left something really important behind, and I didn't like the feeling," Mac confessed.

"I was panicked when I woke up and you weren't here. I felt this loss come over me again until… well, until I saw your note."

"Brad, I'm so sorry. I should have thought of that. But you were sleeping so soundly, and I know how hard it's been for you to sleep. I just didn't want to wake you."

"You're a good man, Mac, and I don't know what I would do without you."

"I'm sure you'd be just fine, but let's hope you never have to find out," Mac said.

"And…." Mac said, "You've been holding out on me, Bradford."

"What do you mean?" Brad asked.

"Where did you learn to use a VHF radio like that?" Mac asked. "I was planning on giving you a few basic lessons before I left, but I forgot. Now I see you didn't really need them."

"Oh that," Brad said. "My parents had a small yacht when I was a teenager, and my dad taught me to use the radio in case of an emergency."

"He did a great job. You're really good at it," Mac said.

"It just all came back to me," Brad confessed. "And while we're talking about the radio, it has really good range. I heard you radio air traffic control for a request to land at Lake Hood."

"Really," Mac said with a surprised look on his face. "What else did you hear?" he asked.

"Now, let me see," Brad said. "I heard you asked to switch to channel thirty-eight, and… of course, I switched to channel thirty-eight."

Brad looked at Mac, who was getting a little red in the face.

"I heard Dan try to set you up with a divorcée and…."

Mac really started to blush.

"I heard you say that you were seeing someone."

"Okay, I've heard enough," Mac said.

Brad started to laugh. "I didn't know you were seeing anyone. When did this happen?"

"Very funny," Mac said.

"No, really, where do you find the time?" Brad asked.

"Stop it, Brad," Mac said with a slight grin. "I just didn't want to be fixed up, that's all."

"Oh, I was hoping that 'someone' you were talking about was me," Brad said.

Mac smiled. "You were?"

"Yep," Brad said. "But if it all had to do with you not wanting to be fixed up, then I guess I was wrong."

"No, Brad, you weren't wrong," Mac said. "But I don't know where it came from. I mean, it just came out. I guess subconsciously I wanted it to be true, and I really wanted it to be you."

"Mac, I want that too."

Mac relaxed for the first time since this conversation had started. He leaned in and gently brushed his lips against Brad's.

Brad put his hand around the back of Mac's neck and pulled him further into the kiss. Mac pressed his tongue against Brad's lips, and Brad opened up to him. Mac's warm mouth tasted of brandy and breath mints.

Mac pulled away and set his brandy glass on the table, and took Brad's from his hand and did the same. He leaned back into Brad and gently laid him down on the couch. Again he put his lips on Brad's, and Brad again opened up to him. They explored the inside of each other's mouths as their tongues danced around in ecstasy. They could both feel their growing erections through their thin pajama bottoms, and Brad was the first to grind his erection into Mac's. Mac responded in like, and they humped each other, both hesitant, but not wanting to stop. Brad ran his fingers through Mac's thick, coal-black hair and caressed his neck and back. Mac had both arms around Brad's back in a death grip, as if he never wanted to let go.

Suddenly, one of the open shutters slammed shut and scared them back into reality.

"Oh shit," Mac said. "I'll get it."

He jumped off of the couch and opened the front door. Wind and snow filled the small cabin within seconds. Mac pushed his way outside to the porch and closed both sets of shutters. By the time

Brad made it to the front door, Mac was already coming back in and pushing against the door to get it closed.

"You're covered in snow, Mac. Let's get you out of those wet clothes before you freeze to death."

Brad pulled Mac's dampened T-shirt over his head and stopped cold when he saw Mac's chiseled pectoral muscles and washboard abdomen.

"My God, Mac, you're beautiful."

Mac smiled and shyly said, "Thanks."

"Take your pants and socks off while I get you some dry clothes."

Mac did as he was told while Brad went to his dresser and retrieved another long-sleeved T-shirt, a pair of pajama bottoms, and another pair of socks.

When Mac had the T-shirt and pants on, they headed for the couch.

Brad wrapped a blanket around Mac's shoulders and gently pushed him down on one end of the couch and stretched his legs out the length of the couch.

He handed Mac his brandy and said, "We need to get you warmed up."

"I'll be fine in a minute," Mac said as he took a sip of his brandy.

Brad lifted Mac's legs and slid in under them. He rubbed Mac's feet with his warm hands and one by one put on his dry socks.

"Thanks, Brad," Mac said. "It's been a long time since anyone has taken care of me, and to be honest, it feels pretty good."

"I like taking care of you, Mac. It feels good and somehow right. Mac?"

"Yeah?"

"About what we were doing before the interruption."

"What about it?"

"I was really enjoying it, and I want to do it again soon, but can we take things slowly? I mean, I know what I'm feeling for you, but I don't know what I'm feeling about how I feel about you. Does that make any sense?"

"I totally understand," Mac said. "I feel the same way. This is still all so new to me."

"So we're on the same page?" Brad asked.

"I think so, and when the time is right, I think we'll both know it."

Brad continued to warm Mac's cold feet until they were again as toasty as they had been. Mac opened his legs as an invitation for Brad to join him on his end of the couch, and Brad gladly accepted.

Brad nestled into Mac and laid his head and back on Mac's chest, feeling at home there with Mac's arms wrapped tightly around him. They spent the day in that position, sipping brandy, snacking on junk food, and napping as the storm raged outside their little cabin.

chapter 21 ✈

MAC opened his eyes, and it was very dark and chilly in the cabin. At some point, Brad had turned over and was now sleeping with his head on Mac's shoulder and his arm draped over his chest. He liked the secure feeling, and tightened his grip around Brad's shoulders and back. Brad stirred a little at Mac's movement, but snuggled in even closer.

Mac said, "Wake up, Bradford. We've been napping all day." The winds appeared to have died down some, but were still howling at a steady clip.

"What time is it?" Brad mumbled.

Mac lifted his arm and looked at this wristwatch.

"Five thirty," he responded.

"Wow, we have slept the day away. I don't want to get up. It's so warm, snuggled up here on the couch," Brad said.

"I know what you mean," Mac said. "But if we don't get the fire going again, we'll freeze to death."

"My head knows you're right, but my body is still saying no."

"Okay," Mac said. "You stay here, and I'll get the fire going again."

"No can do," Brad said. "We'll do it together."

The shutters being closed made it seem like nighttime.

"It's pretty dark in here," Brad said. "I'll get the lamps going, and you get the fire going again."

"Deal," Mac replied.

They got up, Mac headed for the fireplace while Brad made his rounds, lighting the oil lamps. When the fire was roaring again and the cabin was starting to get toasty, Mac opened the front door to a wall of snow. He couldn't really tell if it was just drifts or if it had snowed that much. He quickly closed the door again and ran back to the couch.

"We've got quite a bit of digging out tomorrow morning if we're ever going to get out of here," Mac said.

Brad was in the kitchen taking a mental inventory of food. "Tomorrow's tomorrow," he said. "How about lasagna for dinner tonight?"

Mac jumped off of the couch and walked to the kitchen. "Sounds good to me. What can I do to help?"

"You can get the stove going if you don't mind," Brad asked.

"Are you sure?" Mac asked. "You remember what happened the last time I loaded the stove with wood."

Brad chuckled. "Yes, I do, but this time, just don't put too much wood in the firebox."

"Yes sir," he said with a military salute.

Mac got the stove started, opened a bottle of red wine, and poured each of them a glass. He put Brad's glass down on the counter beside Brad and sat down at the little kitchen table. Mac simply watched as Brad stood at the counter, silently building his lasagna.

I can't believe the turn my life has taken over the last six months, but it sure does feel pretty good, he thought.

Brad turned around and saw Mac was deep in thought. "What's going on in that head of yours, flyboy?" he asked.

Mac snapped out of his daydream. "Oh, nothing really. I just can't believe where my life has taken me in the last six months."

"I know what you mean, but is that a good thing or a bad thing?" Brad asked.

"A good thing, I think. I'm still sorting through a lot of questions about myself, but I like where I am right now. How about you?"

"I'm still missing Jeff, but you make that so much easier, and like you, I also like where I am right now. This feels pretty damn good."

"So, we're still on the same page. That's good," Mac said.

"And I think as long as we're open with our thoughts and feelings and keep communicating, we'll keep it that way," Brad said.

"I agree," Mac said.

"Oh, I forgot to tell you. When I was in Anchorage, I talked to Jack. He wants to come up for a few days when I pick up Zander and Jake in a week. Is that okay with you?"

"Sure, Mac, but you don't need to ask my permission. This place is half yours too, remember."

"Thanks, but you spend more time here than I do, and this is your only home right now, so I just wanted to make sure you were okay with it," Mac said.

"I really appreciate that, and thanks for asking, but your family is welcome here anytime."

"No thanks needed," Mac said. "You know, I never really told you why I was so anxious to buy this place with you."

"I thought it was because of my good looks and charming personality," Brad said.

"Well, of course that was part of it—how could it not be?" Mac said through a big smile. "But when I first started working for Zander and Jake and flew the rented plane, occasionally Lindsey would make a trip with me, and we would spend the night at the lodge. We would hike up this very trail sometimes, and one day we stumbled on this cabin, just like you did."

That got Brad's attention. "This cabin?" he asked.

"One and the same," he said.

Brad put the lasagna in the oven and sat across from Mac at the table. "That's amazing, Mac."

"Of course, it wasn't for sale then, but we always dreamed of having a place like this. I had forgotten all about it until you mentioned that there was a cabin you wanted to buy. And I wasn't really certain it was even the same cabin until we got here. So much has changed over the years. It didn't have running water or solar power at the time, and there was an outhouse out back. It was so rustic, I fell in love with it that very minute. And I am so grateful to you for making me a part of it."

"Mac, I am really happy I could be part of a dream of yours. I know Lindsey would be happy for you too."

"I hope so," Mac said. "I also hope she would be okay with this." He gestured to the two of them.

"There really isn't a *this* yet, Mac, but you know Lindsey would want you to be happy, and if and when there *is* a this and it makes you happy, then I think she would be all for it," Brad said.

"I wish I could be sure," Mac said as his eyes started to fill with tears.

"Mac, nothing is a sure thing in life, and we both know that better than anyone. Do you think I ever imagined, in my wildest dreams, that I would be thirty-eight years old and starting my life over, without Jeff in it?" Brad asked.

"Of course not," Mac said. "Neither of us did, but this is the hand we were dealt. I was forty when I lost Lindsey, and I had the same fears that you have right now. But think about this. After dealing with the loss of my wife, I'm about to turn forty-six in a couple of months, and I'm just now realizing that I may be gay. How's that for a life-changing experience?" Mac asked.

"I understand, Mac, but please don't feel like anyone's pushing you to do or be anything that you're not. Take all the time you need, and the answer will come to you."

Mac reached over and grabbed Brad's hand.

"I hope you're right, because it feels really good just being with you," Mac said.

"I know how good it feels. I'm here too, remember? But we can't live the rest of our lives locked away in this cabin. If we end up together, and that's a big if… people are going to know about it. That includes Zander and Jake, Jack and Zoe-Grace, and anyone else that we know. You will be in a relationship with a man, and there will be no turning back. You can't expect me to live my life as a lie. That's not fair to me, and it's certainly not fair to you," Brad said.

"You're right, Brad. And if and when I make a commitment to you, I don't give a damn about what anyone thinks, except Jack and Zoe. Jack's like my brother, and, well, Zoe-Grace, she goes without saying. I don't want to lose either of them."

"Mac, if Jack and Zoe truly love you, they will accept you as you are. What if it was the other way around, and Jack or Zoe was telling you that he or she was gay, would you care any less for them?"

"I hope that I wouldn't," Mac said. He stood and started to pace. "I've been around Zander and Jake forever, and you and Jeff for the last five years too. Have I ever given you any reason to believe that I had anything against your lifestyle?"

"No, you haven't, but listen to yourself. You just said 'your' as in 'our' lifestyle. And now we may be talking about your lifestyle as well. Is it still okay?"

"I guess that's what I have to figure out. I would love to say that it wouldn't matter, but I just don't know."

Mac walked around the back of Brad's chair and put his arms around his neck and buried his face in Brad's neck. He whispered, "All I know is that I am here with you because I want to be. I don't know what that means or what kind of label to put on it. I just know I want to be here with you."

Brad reached over his shoulder and cupped the back of Mac's head and ran his fingers through his hair.

"That's enough for me right now, Mac. I can't judge you. Hell, I don't have anything better to offer you right now either."

The kitchen timer Brad had set when he put the lasagna in the oven dinged, interrupting the tender moment. Mac straightened up to allow Brad to stand and take care of the lasagna. Mac prepared a loaf of garlic bread and placed it in the oven, and then moved on to the salad. When he was through tossing the salad and the bread was ready, Brad sliced and served the lasagna, and Mac served the salad and cut the bread.

Before they sat down, Mac lit a candle for the table and put on his favorite Dinah Washington CD. Brad poured them each another glass of wine, and they settled down to eat. During dinner the conversation stayed light and fun. Brad teased Mac mercilessly about his singing, and Mac gave it right back to him about running him down while Brad was skipping down the mountain like Maria Von Trapp in *The Sound of Music*. They laughed and talked for a couple of hours before they finally got up to clear the table and wash the dishes.

Brad was washing dishes, and Mac was waiting to dry when Dinah started singing "What A Difference a Day Makes," one of Mac's favorite songs. Mac started singing in a low sexy voice.

"'What a difference a day made, Twenty-four little hours…'"

Mac moved in behind Brad and put his arms around his waist. He started swaying while he sang. Brad dried his hands and turned around in Mac's arms. Brad took the lead as he attempted to dance with Mac. Mac stopped singing and hesitated for only a second, then followed Brad's lead. Mac sang as Brad spun him around.

The song ended, but they kept dancing.

"This feels so weird," Mac said as "This Bitter Earth" was next out of the little boom box.

"What?" Brad whispered.

"Dancing with a guy."

"Why does it feel weird?" Brad asked.

"For one thing, I've never followed before, so that's part of it. But girls are so fragile, soft, and light on their feet, and you are, well... masculine and strong... and to be honest, a little heavy on yours."

"Well, we'll stop," Brad said as he stopped dancing and dropped his hands down to his side.

"Don't get your panties in a wad, I'm just kidding," Mac said.

This time Mac took the lead, and they started dancing again.

"Now, this feels much better," Mac said.

"Okay then, I guess that settles it; you're the leader," Brad whispered again. "I guess I can live with that," he said.

"Good, now shut up and dance with me," Mac said through a plastered-on smile.

They danced around the little cabin to every song left on the CD. When the music stopped, Brad looked at his watch.

"Mac, it's one thirty in the morning."

"Are you kidding me?" Mac asked.

"Nope, we have to go to bed. We have a lot to do tomorrow."

They went through their routine, getting the cabin ready for the night. In ten minutes, the fire was blazing, and the oil lamps were out. They both hit the bathroom and brushed their teeth and washed up. When they were finished, they stood in the middle of the living room.

"What now?" Mac asked.

"Mac, would you like to bunk in with me again?"

"I'd like that very much, if you want me to. I mean... it's a great way to stay warm," Mac replied with a wink and a smile.

"Mac," Brad said.

"What?"

"Get in bed."

"Whatever you say, Brad."

They both stripped down to their T-shirts and boxers and climbed into bed. They assumed the same positions they'd done the previous night, and before Brad could say good night, he heard Mac's very light snoring. He settled and tightened Mac's arms around his waist and simply listened. Eventually, he fell off into a peaceful slumber.

BRAD woke up sometime later to Mac getting out of bed. He sat up and turned over to see if Mac was okay, but it wasn't Mac. It was Jeff.

"Hey, buddy," Jeff said.

"Jeff?" Brad said. "Is it really you?"

"In the flesh, sort of," Jeff replied.

"When... how did you get here?" Brad said. "Oh my God, you look great. Are you okay?"

"I'm really well, Brad. It's amazing to feel this good."

"How long can you stay? I've missed you so much, Jeff," Brad said.

"I can't stay, and besides, you're doing great for yourself. You got a good man taking care of you," Jeff said.

"You know about Mac? Are you mad at me?" Brad asked.

"Of course not, Brad. I made you promise me before I died that you would go on with your life and try to be happy," Jeff said.

"Yeah, but it's only been six months," Brad said as he looked a little embarrassed. "Jeff, you know me well enough to know I didn't come up here expecting to get involved with a straight man. All this sort of just happened. And to be honest, I really don't know what to think about it all."

"I know, Brad, it's okay. I know without a doubt that you loved me, and believe me when I say that I knew everything that was going on around me when I died. I know you climbed up in bed with me. I left this earth in your arms. It meant everything to me."

Jeff reached over and gently kissed Brad on the lips.

"But just know it's time to let me go. We're in different places now, but someday we will be together again, and I exist for that time. But in the meantime, you need to live. Mac is a good man, and he cares for you. He might not know it yet, but he's in love with you."

Brad tried to interrupt, and Jeff put his finger on Brad's lips to stop him.

"You need to be patient with Mac and try to understand that he has had such a short time to deal with these new emotions. It will all work out in the end. Everything always happens as it's supposed to. I will always love you, and Mac loves you too. Just remember that."

Brad rolled over to get out of bed, and when he turned around, Jeff was gone.

"No, wait, I have so many questions. I love you too, Jeff. No, come back!"

Brad felt himself being shaken and heard someone saying, "Wake up, Brad."

"Brad, wake up. Brad?"

Brad opened his eyes, and Mac was holding him.

"Brad, please wake up," Mac pleaded.

"Mac?"

"Brad, you were having a dream," Mac said.

"I know." Brad held on to Mac tighter and kissed his neck and face.

"Brad, are you okay?" Mac asked.

"I'm okay now, thanks to you," Brad said.

"What do you mean?" Mac asked.

Brad told him about Jeff and the dream and everything Jeff had said to him.

"Wow, that's some dream. So what now?" Mac asked.

"Mac, I think Jeff came to me because he knew I was struggling with having feelings for you and not wanting to let him go. I think he came to me to give me his blessing," Brad said with tears in his eyes.

Mac again took Brad in his arms and held him tight.

"Mac, if and when you're ready to explore something with me, I'm here, ready, and waiting," Brad whispered into Mac's ear.

Mac held him even tighter as they slid down into bed and settled in for the night.

Mac was very glad it was dark in the cabin, so Brad couldn't see the fear on his face. It was one thing if they both weren't sure what they wanted, but now Brad knew exactly what he wanted, and Mac was still unsure. Would this change things between them?

chapter 22

THE next morning, Brad woke first and slid out of bed, careful not to wake Mac. Mac had had a very restless night, and Brad had a pretty good idea why. He fumbled around the cabin, trying to make coffee and put together a little breakfast to take to Mac in bed.

When breakfast was ready, he filled a tray with enough coffee, bagels and cream cheese, and a fruit salad for two. He made his way quietly back to bed, put the tray on the bedside table, and slipped under the covers.

"Good morning, flyboy," he whispered into Mac's ear.

Mac slowly opened his eyes and smiled. He stretched and yawned and said, "Good morning."

Brad gently kissed him on the cheek and said, "I made breakfast."

Mac looked over Brad's shoulder and saw the tray on the bedside table.

"Do you want to start with coffee?" Brad asked.

"That would be amazing," Mac mumbled.

Brad poured them each a cup and passed one to Mac. Mac scooted up a little and rested his back and head on the bed's headboard. Brad followed his lead, and they sipped their coffees.

Brad put his cup of coffee down and turned to face Mac. "Mac, you were pretty restless last night. I know you didn't sleep very well, and I think I have a pretty good idea why."

Mac looked at Brad with a quizzical expression. "Let's hear it," Mac said.

"Promise me that you will hear me out before you interrupt, okay?" Brad asked. "I need to get this out."

Mac nodded while still sipping his coffee.

"Last night, when you woke me after my dream and I explained everything that Jeff had tried to communicate to me, you seemed to have that 'deer in the headlights' look. I wasn't really thinking clearly, or I wouldn't have said anything about being ready for *this*." He used his index finger to point back and forth between the two of them. "Mac, I'm sorry."

Mac started to speak, and Brad stopped him. "Please, let me finish," he told him. Mac closed his mouth and nodded again.

"When you and I were figuring out things between us and we were both on the fence about how, when, or if we should pursue this friendship, relationship, whatever you want to call it, we were on a level playing field.

"Now that I've decided I want to explore this, the field is no longer level. That must feel like an awful lot of pressure on you, and I want to take that pressure away, Mac. You don't deserve any pressure from me and you won't get any. You've been a lifesaver, and I can never ever thank you enough for pulling me through this terrible loss and showing me life can go on. But... if you walked out of this cabin today, I would be upset and very sad, but I wouldn't go after you. This is your decision to make, with no strings attached. I know now that I will survive, and I owe that secure feeling to you."

Brad set the cup with what was left of his cold coffee on the bedside table and stood. He walked to the foot of the bed and crossed his arms over his chest.

"So here's the deal. The way I see it, this could go a couple different ways. The first scenario would be that we pursue this thing and see where it goes. If it works, we live happily ever after. If it doesn't, we remain friends and keep the cabin and go on as we have been. If you choose not to do that, then I'll buy you out, no questions asked and no hard feelings, and we go our separate ways. You could also decide that you don't even want to try, and with that decision, the other endings will also apply. Either way, we're both going to be okay."

Mac looked at Brad as if begging to speak with his eyes.

"Okay, you can speak now."

Mac patted the empty spot on the bed next to him.

"Come back and sit here next to me," he said. "Yes, I was restless, but not for the reasons you think—well, not all of them anyway. Yeah, it does feel like a little more pressure, but not from you. It's all self-inflicted. Last night, I thought a lot about what you said about always knowing you were gay and your theory regarding people being born sexual, and it all kind of makes sense in an odd sort of way."

"Thanks," Brad said.

"Now let me finish," Mac said.

Brad threw up his hands in an "I'm sorry, you're right" kind of gesture.

"I haven't always thought I was gay. In fact, I never thought I was gay, but here I am with feelings and an attraction to a man—not just any man, Brad, but you."

Now it was Mac's time to fidget. He sat up a little straighter and smoothed out the sheets on top of his legs.

"I tried to figure out why God or the universe, whichever you believe in, would bring us together and allow these feelings to surface without allowing us to act on them. I loved Lindsey with all of my heart, and if she were still alive, this would never have been an issue, but she's not alive, and I'm alone, except for Jack and Zoe. Then I thought that maybe we were brought together five years ago, when you and Jeff started coming up to the lake, in preparation for all this—you, dealing with Jeff's death and my needing someone in my life. It's all so far-fetched, but how else can you explain it?"

"My sentiments exactly," Brad added.

"Brad, I guess what I'm trying to say is, yes, I want to explore this thing and see where it goes. I just need to go slow and get used to it a little at a time. Does that make sense?"

"It makes perfect sense," Brad said. "That's some heavy shit. No wonder you were restless," Brad said.

Brad took the cup of coffee out of Mac's hands and put it down. He snuggled into Mac and laid his head on Mac's chest. Mac wrapped his arms around Brad, and they lay there in silence.

"No pressure, Mac. All on your terms and timing," Brad whispered. "I have all the time in the world and nowhere to go."

Mac squeezed him tighter and kissed the top of his head. Brad looked up at Mac, and their lips met. Brad welcomed Mac's tongue, and again they explored each other. Brad pulled away from the kiss, not wanting to push.

"How about some breakfast?" Brad asked.

"Sure, after all that deep thinking, I'm really hungry."

They shared breakfast and another cup of coffee, smooching in between bits and sips and simply enjoying each other's company in the early morning hours.

The cabin was still very dark due to the closed shutters, but they were both anxious to see how much snow had fallen and if there was any damage.

"Up and at 'em," Mac said as he pulled the covers back and hopped out of bed. "We have a lot to do today, and the day's half over."

Brad followed Mac's lead, and they both ran for the bathroom. Mac made it there first, because he was smaller-built and slimmer, whereas Brad was taller, bulkier, and more muscular.

Brad waited outside for a minute, and then put his fist to the door.

"What are you doing in there?" he yelled. "A beauty regimen?"

Through a mouth full of toothpaste, he heard Mac yell, "I'm brushing my teeth."

Brad opened the door and stepped up to the sink. "If that's all, there's no reason why we can't do that together."

Mac smiled, toothpaste running down his chin as Brad squeezed the tube onto his toothbrush and ran it under the running water. Mac brushed with one hand and slid the other behind Brad's waist as they stood, side by side, brushing their teeth.

When they were both finished in the bathroom and dressed, they walked to the front door and stopped.

"Here we go," Mac said.

"I feel like Thelma and Louise," Brad replied.

Mac chuckled and said, "You ready?"

"Go for it."

Mac opened the door, and all they saw was white. They closed the door and walked to the back door and did the same. More white.

"How do we get out?" Brad asked.

"We dig," Mac replied.

Mac grabbed the two snow shovels he'd placed inside the back door yesterday, and they started pushing the snow outward from the top down. When Mac realized the snow was solid, they stopped and closed the door.

"Let's try the front door," Mac said. "The storm came in from the south, which is why the back porch is covered. The front porch should be mostly drifts."

They again opened the front door and repeated the process. After a couple of minutes, they could both see bright blue sky. They continued digging until they could get out of the door and start on the porch itself. The solid snow was about level with the front porch, which was about four feet off the ground, so clearing the front porch wasn't too bad. But as they made their way around the side of the wraparound porch, the back porch was a different story. The rear of the cabin was level with the ground, which made it much more difficult to clear.

When they stopped for lunch, Mac made grilled cheese sandwiches and tomato soup while Brad carried the rocking chairs from the living room and put them back in their spots. They ate, staring at the amazing view of the snow-covered mountains and terrain. Mac could barely make out his plane, but it seemed to be okay. Tomorrow they would hike down the mountain and check on the lodge and the plane and make their way back up before dinner.

After lunch and another five hours of shoveling, the back porch was clear and a path to the storage shed was dug, so they could get at their snowshoes and other equipment. When they finally gave up for the day, it was six thirty. They were both beat. Mac dropped onto the couch and attempted to get his snow boots off.

"Let me help," Brad said. "Then you can help me with mine."

"Deal," Mac said as he lifted his booted foot into the air.

Brad unlaced Mac's left boot and pulled it off. Mac's foot was ice-cold and soaking wet. He stripped off Mac's sock; his foot was as shriveled as if he'd been in the swimming pool all day. Brad warmed Mac's foot between his hands for a few minutes, then started on his right foot. He followed the same procedure, and shortly Mac was removing his ski pants and sweatshirt. Brad stopped a minute just to watch the strip show, and noticed how hot Mac looked in his long silk ski underwear.

When Mac finished getting the cold, wet clothes off, he motioned for Brad to sit on the couch. He did the same to Brad, and soon they were sitting on the couch side by side, out of breath, with a pile of wet clothes on the floor.

Mac stood first to stoke the small fire and put more wood on it, as Brad got up to get the bottle of brandy. It had gotten too cold for beer, and besides, the brandy had a great warming effect. They sipped brandy while they discussed the chores of the day and a plan for tomorrow.

"I think I need a hot shower to take the chill off," Brad said. "Do you mind if I go first?" he asked.

"Of course not, help yourself."

Brad walked into the bathroom, but didn't close the door. Mac watched as Brad turned the shower on and started to remove his long underwear. When he was naked, he stood waiting for the water to get hot.

Out of the corner of his eye, Brad could see Mac staring at him. Mac didn't turn away when Brad removed his shirt, so Brad stood there a little longer than he needed to, flexing his biceps and tightening his abs. He figured if Mac was curious, he would help him out. So Brad took his time removing his underwear. *This would be the real test*, he thought. He slowly removed his long underwear one leg at a time, and when he was totally naked, he stood there waiting for the water to heat up. He turned slightly so Mac had a clear view of him without looking too obvious. Mac didn't turn away. In fact, he appeared to be studying Brad's dick. The thought of that started to get Brad excited, and he didn't want Mac to see him with an erection, so he quickly stepped into the shower.

Mac watched Brad intently, not knowing if Brad could see him or not. He felt voyeuristic, and it excited him just a bit. Mac had never seen Brad naked before, and he was beautiful. Mac stared at Brad's finely chiseled chest and made his way down to his tight, washboard abs. He stopped when his gaze reached Brad's dick. He had never actually looked at another man's dick, except at the gym, like most guys do when they take a quick glance to make sure they are still on the average size. But he surprised himself as he studied Brad's dick and compared it to his own. Brad was circumcised, as was he. He was very long, at least an inch or so longer than his own, and just as thick as he was. Brad pulled back the shower curtain and stepped in. The show was over, and if he was honest with himself, Mac was disappointed. He wondered if size mattered to guys and blushed a little at the thought. He wasn't sure if it was the brandy or seeing Brad naked, but he got up from the couch and walked into the bathroom, undressed, and stepped into the shower with Brad.

Brad simply smiled and said, "Hey, flyboy," when Mac stepped into the shower.

"You mind if I join you?" Mac asked.

"Not at all," Brad responded.

Brad stepped aside to allow Mac to get some of the hot water. He lathered up a washcloth and began to wash Mac's back. Mac seemed to melt into the touch and seemed more relaxed than he had been in a while. When he was through with Mac's back, he worked his way down to his butt. Mac tensed up a little, and Brad said, "Relax, I'm not going to do anything to make you uncomfortable. If you become uncomfortable, just say stop, and I will."

Mac nodded in approval.

Brad washed each buttock, massaging as he went. He went down on his knees and washed Mac's legs one at a time, and then his feet. He moved back up and washed Mac's neck and whispered, "Turn around."

Mac did as he was told, and Brad lightly kissed him on the lips. He washed his chest and moved down to his groin. He dropped the washcloth and soaped up his hand. Mac was already partially hard, and he slowly touched Mac's dick. Brad was watching Mac's face, and Mac closed his eyes.

"Mac, open your eyes," Brad whispered. "I want you to see that it's me pleasuring you, not anyone else."

Mac opened his eyes and smiled. "I know exactly who you are," he whispered.

Brad continued to stroke Mac's now fully engorged cock, and Mac again melted into the motion. Mac picked up the soap and lathered his hands and hesitantly touched Brad's erect dick. They stood face to face, with the hot water creating a steamy effect in the tiny bathroom while they stroked each other's hard cocks.

Mac placed his hand around Brad's neck and gently pulled him in for a long kiss. Brad opened for him, as he began to breathe harder and harder. Mac, sensing that Brad was close, picked up the pace as Brad moaned into this mouth. Brad jerked and flailed as the spasms hit, and he released his load while still stroking Mac. Mac felt his balls drawing up and started making the same moaning sounds and tightening his grip on Brad's neck. Mac tensed as he shot into Brad's hand. Mac slowed his breathing, gently bit Brad's bottom lip, and held on, resting his forehead on Brad's.

When their lips parted, Brad whispered, "That was amazing."

"I'll say," Mac said with a shy grin.

The water was starting to get cold, so Mac said, "Let's get out of here and into a warm bed."

"I'm all for that," Brad replied.

Mac stepped out first and started drying off. Brad stood in the cool shower, wrapping his arms around himself to keep warm. When Mac was dry, he gestured for Brad to step out, and he was waiting with a dry towel. Mac started drying Brad from head to toe, not seeming to be embarrassed in the least. He dried Brad's chest, then his back and neck and made his way down to his dick and butt. He parted Brad's butt cheeks and dried the area thoroughly and lifted his dick and dried his balls and moved down to both legs and feet.

When they were both dry, they ran from the bathroom to Brad's bed and jumped in. They held on to each other tightly until they were again warm and comfortable. Mac took a deep breath and jumped out of the bed. He grabbed a bottle of wine, two glasses, and the wine opener and then ran back to the bed and slipped back under the covers. He opened the wine, poured them each a glass, stuck the cork back in the bottle, and put the bottle on the floor.

"Brad, that was incredible," Mac said as he sipped his wine.

Brad smiled. "It *was* incredible, but I've gotta say, I was a little surprised when you climbed into the shower with me."

"You weren't more surprised than I was," Mac said. "I just did it and didn't think about it. You know, it wasn't the least bit strange. In fact, it was the best hand job I've ever had, no offense to Lindsey. It's like you just knew what I liked and what felt good."

"I know what you mean," Brad said. "I just did what feels good to me, and you pretty much did the same thing. Two guys have that connection that a man and woman don't really have. Guys can never know what it feels like for a woman or what feels good because we don't have a vagina. But all guys have dicks, and dicks pretty much work the same way."

Mac released such a lighthearted laugh that Brad couldn't help but laugh too.

"I have a confession to make," Mac said. "I was really worried about the first time. I mean, I had very little doubt that there would be a first time, but I was scared shitless."

"I was nervous as well," Brad admitted. "Unlike you, I didn't know if there would ever be a first time, and to be honest, I haven't been intimate with anyone but Jeff for fifteen years. That's some pressure, and the fact that you had never been intimate with a man made me even more nervous as hell."

"I'm glad the first time is behind us, so we can focus on the fun," Mac said.

"Amen, brother," Brad responded. "Mac?"

"Yes, Bradford."

"In time, I want to show you things and have you experience everything the male body has to offer. It can be quite intoxicating sometimes," Brad said. "Would you be open to that?"

"Bradford, I trust you completely, and I know you would never intentionally make me uncomfortable, but just do me a favor and take it easy with me at first, and give me some time to adjust to all this. We have all the time in the world to explore each other's bodies, and for the first time since this all started, I'm looking forward to getting to know all of you."

"I totally understand, and I'll be gentle with you, flyboy," Brad said. "Now, I'm damn hungry. What do you say I heat up the leftover lasagna?"

"I say go for it, and I'll stay here and watch you do it," Mac said.

"Very funny," Brad said as he slipped on some sweats and a T-shirt.

"Damn," Mac said. "I thought you were going to do it naked."

"Hell no!" Brad shouted. "It's so damn cold in here there would be major shrinkage."

Mac laughed so hard he spit red wine all over the bed. When he'd composed himself, he said, "Glad this is your bed. It's full of wine stains now."

"My bed, huh?" Brad asked. "If it's my bed, why've you had your butt in it for the last few days?"

"'Cause your butt was in it," he replied.

"Good answer. Now light some of those oil lamps, so I can see you."

"You're bossy," Mac yelled while he was on his way to the fireplace.

"I am not bossy. I just want to be able to see you running around here naked, doing your chores."

"Okay," Mac said. "Then naked you get."

When dinner was ready, they got back in bed and ate lasagna and sipped wine until they were well sated. They got out of bed just long enough to do the dishes and open another bottle of wine. When the kitchen was cleaned and the sheets changed, they were tucked back into bed with wine glass in hand, they settled down and relaxed.

After five minutes of comfortable silence, Mac reached over and put his wine glass on the table and did the same with Brad's. He snuggled into Brad, laid his head on Brad's chest, and rubbed his washboard stomach.

"How do you get that tight stomach and keep it?" Mac asked.

"Good genes, I think. I haven't worked out seriously in five years, but I do watch what I eat, not that you can tell by the way we eat up here. If you remember, when Jeff first died, I didn't really have an appetite for several weeks, and that kept the weight off, but if I keep eating like this and going to bed, I'll be as big as this cabin."

"I wish I had good genes," Mac said. "I usually work out three to four times a week, and I still struggle with the weight and the love handles."

"You're in great shape, Mac. Maybe you can bring up some workout equipment, and we can set up a little gym in the corner. It would be fun to work out with you."

"I can do that," Mac said. "It will take a few trips because of the weight load issues, but I think I can manage it."

"That sounds great," Brad said.

"Bradford?"

"Yeah, Mac."

"I really like lying like this, with my head on your chest and feeling your strong, hard body underneath mine. You know, with Lindsey, I was always the man and always had to be the strong one. Not that she made me feel that way or anything, but just because I always thought that's what the man was supposed to do. But with two guys, we can share being strong, and that's really nice."

"It is nice, Mac, and you are so right. You're really catching on to this man-to-man thing."

"Does that make me gay?" Mac asked.

"No labels, remember? We are what we are, Mac, and we owe it to ourselves to be what we are. At least what we are right now."

"What do you mean by 'right now'?" Mac asked.

"Mac, come on, I'm not fooling myself into thinking that you'll always be here with me. In my opinion, most people who are truly bisexual can never be exclusively with a man or a woman for any period of time, because at some point, they want the other sex," Brad explained.

"If your theory holds," Mac said, "maybe Lindsey was just someone I fell in love with because we were alike and had some sort of bond, sort of like we do, regardless of her sex," Mac said.

"Maybe," Brad said. "But I'm not saying my theory's bulletproof. I think that some men and women fall in love with the opposite sex because they believe that's the only acceptable option. I also think that some men and women fall in love with the opposite or, in many cases, the same sex because that's their preference. The unlucky ones who choose the same sex, do so knowing that society will always frown upon them and make them feel unworthy. I'm not sure which category you fall into, but if it's the latter, I'm really in trouble."

Mac thought about what Brad had said before he spoke next.

"You know, Lindsey was the first and last woman I ever wanted to be with, and I've never been attracted to a man until you, so where does that put me?" Mac asked.

"Who knows, Mac? The one thing I do know is that Jeff's death taught me that I want to live each day like it was my last. I want to enjoy the time I have with you right now, because we'll never know what tomorrow will bring. If we can't learn anything from the pain we experienced from losing our spouses, we're hopeless."

"Wow, Bradford," Mac said. "Very well put." He tilted his head up to Brad's. Brad met his lips in a deep passionate kiss. Brad rolled over and pinned Mac beneath him.

Brad captured Mac's face in his hands and looked into his eyes. He saw what he thought was fear and desire.

"You okay, Mac? You want me to stop?" he whispered.

Mac mouthed "No," and began to tremble a little, but held on to Brad.

He whispered into Mac's ear, "Remember, if you're uncomfortable, just say stop, and I'll stop. No expectations and no disappointments."

Mac nodded as Brad went in for a deeper kiss. Mac ran his fingers through Brad's hair and gripped him tight behind the neck. Brad slid down and encircled Mac's nipple with his tongue. Mac gasped, and Brad bit down lightly and released. Mac arched his back off of the bed. Brad licked across Mac's chest and repeated the same actions on his other nipple, and was rewarded with the same response.

Mac closed his eyes. He was overwhelmed with all the feelings he was experiencing. He couldn't ever remember being this turned on, and that fact frightened him a little. With Lindsey, he had always been the aggressor. But Brad was taking the lead, and he liked it. That thought frightened him even more. He was ripped out of his thoughts by a warm sensation on his dick. Brad had slid down and taken Mac's erect cock into his mouth.

Trembling, Mac mouthed, "Oh God."

Brad took Mac's entire dick in one gulp as it slid down his throat. Mac again came up off the bed and thrust his dick farther down Brad's throat. Brad gagged for an instant, then relaxed, and Mac's dick slid all the way in.

Brad saw that Mac's dick was beautifully shaped, a little shorter than his, but just as thick. He seemed to fit perfectly in Brad's mouth, and Brad wanted so much to pleasure him in every way.

Brad slid his mouth back up and then down again and in the process, tasted Mac's bittersweet juice starting to leak out. *He even tastes beautiful*, Brad thought. Brad went down a few more times, then released Mac's dick and moved down to his balls. He circled each ball with his tongue as he sucked it into his mouth, and then sucked both balls at once and rolled them around in his mouth. He released Mac's balls, lifted his legs, and spread his cheeks to reveal a perfect pink pucker. Knowing what he was about to do was a very personal thing, he reminded himself that all Mac had to do was say stop, and he would stop.

With Mac's legs over his head, Brad went in for the kill. He first tickled Mac's opening lightly with his tongue, then circled it and forced his tongue into the tight opening, over and over again.

Mac grabbed and held his legs in place while he kept moaning and saying, "Oh Brad, oh God, that feels so good."

Brad took such delight in the pleasure he was giving Mac that he was on the verge of coming himself. After one last thrust of his tongue and suckling Mac's pucker, he lowered Mac's legs and engulfed Mac's entire dick in one gulp. He went all the way down and came up once again. He stuck his finger into his mouth and soaked it with saliva and rubbed it around Mac's hole. Mac tensed just a little at the sensation, but as Brad went down again, Mac relaxed.

Mac reached down and grabbed Brad's erect cock and caressed it as he whispered, "Brad, I'm so close." Knowing Mac was at the point of no return, Brad slipped his finger all the way into Mac's tight hole. Again, Mac lifted off of the bed with a loud moan as thrust after thrust of warm cum slid down Brad's throat. Brad was so excited about Mac's reaction and his touch that he came all over Mac's hand the very second he slipped his finger into Mac's hole.

Mac fell back on the bed at the same time Brad slid his finger out of his hole. He lay very still, trying to catch his breath.

Brad asked, "Are you okay, Mac?"

Mac waved a hand as if to say, give me a minute. When he could finally speak, he said, "I'm better than okay. That was incredible."

Brad smiled and climbed off the bed to get a towel to clean himself and Mac.

When he returned with a warm, damp cloth, Mac was in the same position in which he'd left him. Mac opened his eyes and said, "Hey, Bradford, where did you go?"

"To get a clean towel," he said. Mac lay there as Brad wiped him clean of saliva and cum and threw the towel on the floor.

Brad crawled back into bed and slid his arm in under Mac's head and began stroking his hair. Again Mac was curled up with his head on Brad's chest and both arms wrapped tightly around him. Before Brad could say anything, he heard that familiar soft snore to which he'd quickly become accustomed, signaling Mac's slumber. Brad closed his eyes and silently thanked Jeff, God, and the universe for bringing Mac into his life.

chapter 23

BRAD opened his eyes as the light streaked in through the now-opened shutters. At some point in the night, he and Mac had shifted positions and were again spooning, with Mac tucked up tightly behind him. Brad could feel Mac's morning erection poking his back and buttocks, but since they hadn't yet talked about last night, he didn't feel comfortable reaching behind and caressing it.

He looked at the clock, as he always did—*ten forty-five. Wow*, he thought, *we really slept in this morning*. Brad felt Mac begin to run his fingers through his hair in a soft circular motion, and he leaned his head into the touch.

"Morning," Mac whispered.

"Good morning to you," Brad said. "Do you see what time it is?" he asked.

Mac raised his head and looked at the clock. "Wow, I can't tell you the last time I slept until ten forty-five," he said. "But by the looks of the light flooding the cabin, it appears to be a beautiful day."

"That it does," Brad said. "I'll flip you to see who has to get up and make the coffee."

Mac laughed. "Not necessary, I'd love to bring you coffee in bed."

"A man truly after my heart," Brad said.

"After last night, I think I am after your heart, among other things," Mac chuckled.

"About last night," Brad asked. "Are you all right with what happened?"

"Before we talk about last night," Mac said, "let me make the coffee, so I can get back in bed."

"Since you're the one getting up, whatever you say," Brad said.

Mac got out of bed and, surprisingly, didn't bother to put on any clothes. Brad watched Mac's hot, naked body—sporting his morning wood—move around the little kitchen, putting the coffee filter then the coffee into the coffeemaker, filling the glass pot with water, and turning on the brewer. He walked past the bed toward the bathroom and winked at Brad as he passed without saying a word. When he came out of the bathroom, the woody was gone, and he went back to the kitchen. He got out the cream and sugar and placed it on a tray, and since enough coffee had brewed for two cups, he removed the coffee pot from the brewer, filled the cups, and put it back to make the rest of the pot. He was back in bed in eight minutes flat.

He handed Brad his cup and said, "Now, you were saying?"

"I wasn't really saying, I was more asking if you're okay with what happened last night?" Brad asked.

"Hell yeah, I'm okay with it," Mac said. "It was amazing. You were amazing."

Brad smiled.

"And, Brad, I'm really sorry I fell asleep so soon afterwards, I was just so relaxed. It's been so long since I've had that kind of connection with anyone, and I felt so content that I just couldn't help it. I'm really sorry, and I promise it won't happen again."

"Mac, it's okay," Brad said. "Remember, it's women who mostly like the cuddle factor after sex, not men. Don't get me wrong, I love holding you, but I can do that while you sleep. As long as you don't fall asleep during sex, I'll be fine."

"Are you kidding me?" Mac said. "Not a chance of that ever happening. Brad, I never knew sex with a guy could be so hot. I mean, when you started playing with my nipples and did what you did to my ass, man, I thought I was going to fly off the bed. It was so personal, yet so erotic and pleasurable. Who knew? And then when you used your finger, I've never had such an intense orgasm in my life."

"So I gather you're okay with it?" Brad asked.

"Hell yes, I'm okay with it. In fact, I can't wait to do it again," Mac said.

Brad laughed. "Mac, there's so much I want to show you."

And, shyly, Mac said, "Hopefully, I'll be a good student."

"If last night's any indication, I have no doubts," Brad said as he jumped out of bed. "But I've got to pee. Be right back."

When Brad returned, he slid back under the covers against Mac's warm body. By the time they had talked and finished another cup of coffee, it was noon.

Mac reached down and kissed that place he loved so much, in the crook of Brad's neck. He said, "I'd love to stay here all day and do everything we did last night plus a whole lot more, but we promised Zander and Jake that we would go down and check on the lodge, and I really need to check on the plane."

"You're right," Brad said. "Besides, the quicker we get down the mountain, the sooner we can get back up and right back into this spot."

"Amen, brother," Mac said. "Let's get a move on. I have things to learn."

By the time they got ready and suited up in the ski gear, it was almost past lunchtime. Mac made a couple of sandwiches and stuck them in his backpack, along with a couple of bottles of water and a flask of brandy, just as a precaution. Brad tossed his digital camera in the backpack, along with his lightweight collapsible tripod. They strapped their snowshoes to their ski boots, and off they went. Mac took the lead, and from Brad's point of view, the scenery was spectacular—the vistas and Mac. They stopped every so often to take a picture or two, and with Mac unaware, Brad shot photo after photo of him. When they reached the spot where Brad had knocked Mac to the ground, Brad set up the little tripod and the timer on his camera and took their picture with their arms around each other's shoulders.

They made it down the mountain without any trouble, and first checked on the plane. Mac grabbed a push broom from the inside of the plane and brushed all the snow off of the wings, fuselage, and tail. They disconnected the cables securing the plane, curled them up, and placed them under the pilot's seat. Together, they moved the little plane from the beach to the dock in preparation for Mac's trip to get Zander, Jake, and Jack, and then they went to check on the lodge.

They circled the outside of the lodge, and all seemed in good condition. They went inside, took off their ski coats and boots, and while Mac went from room to room, Brad went into the office to use Zander's computer to print off their photos.

Brad had just finished printing the photos and putting them away when Mac found him.

"Are the computers okay?" Mac asked.

"Yep, they seem to be. They must have experienced a power outage or power surge, because the online reservation computer shut down. I rebooted it and I'm just making sure it comes up okay."

The computer beeped and the screen loaded.

"Looks good to me," Brad said as he stood and turned out the light.

They sat in the breakfast room and ate their sandwiches, drank their water, and even took a sip of brandy for the trip back up. When they closed the front door of the lodge, Brad turned, and there was a gleaming red snowmobile waiting for them.

"Your chariot awaits, my good man," Mac said as he bowed and swept his hand toward the machine.

"Really!" Brad said. "You don't think they'll mind?"

"Actually, this is mine," Mac said. "I bought it the first winter I spent any amount of time up here."

"This is so cool," Brad said. "Can I drive?"

"Sure," Mac said. "Just take it easy until you get the feel of her."

Brad climbed in the driver's seat with Mac closely behind him. Before Mac could give Brad any instructions, Brad had the snowmobile started and in gear. He gunned it, and the machine roared as it raced toward the trail. Brad couldn't see it, but Mac had the biggest grin on his face. *Just one more thing I didn't know about this man*, Mac thought.

In a flash they were gone. Brad leaned into every turn like a pro and safely maneuvered the vehicle through the tough terrain. Mac held on for dear life, as the red machine roared its way up the mountain's many twists and turns.

They pulled up to the front of the cabin at five o'clock on the dot. Mac was the first off as he pretended to open a nonexistent door for Brad.

"Chivalry isn't dead after all." Brad chuckled.

"Not on my watch," Mac responded.

Mac climbed back on the snowmobile and pulled it around to the back of the cabin. He secured it in the storage shed and joined Brad in the cabin. Brad had already removed his ski clothes and boots and was bending over, starting the fire, when Mac came up behind him, threw his arms around his waist, and kissed his neck.

"I've wanted to do that all day," he said.

"What stopped you?" Brad asked.

"Oh, I don't know. I guess we were too busy and having too much fun on the snowmobile."

Brad knew it was probably because they weren't in the safety and seclusion of their little cabin, but he wasn't about to get into that now. *Give him time*, he thought.

"Sit on the couch, and let me help you with your boots," Brad said.

Mac did as he was told, and Brad helped him remove both boots. Mac stood and Brad unhooked his ski pants and pulled them down as well. He helped Mac with his coat and sweatshirt, and finally they were down to their long underwear and wool socks.

Mac lit the oil lamps this time while Brad opened a bottle of wine to take the chill off. They sat down next to each other on the couch and sipped their wine.

"So you led me to believe that you had never driven a snowmobile before," Mac said.

"No, I didn't. You just *assumed* that I had never driven a snowmobile," Brad responded. "When we were in Switzerland for Christmas, my parents would rent them and we would take day trips. And when we came here, Jeff and I would use Zander and Jake's and run all over the area. I have such fond memories of all of those times, and now I have one more fond memory of a snowmobile to store away, and luckily, you're in it."

Mac choked up for a second, and when he could finally speak, he said, "It's fun creating memories that will last a lifetime."

"Speaking of memories," Brad said as he reached into the crack of the sofa. "I have something to show you." He handed Mac the photos he had printed off of Zander's computer.

Mac looked at the pictures one by one with a big grin on his face.

"When did you do this?" he asked.

"When we were at the lodge, and you caught me on Zander's computer," Brad said. "I wanted to surprise you, so I made up the cockamamy story about the power going off and on."

As Mac looked through the pictures, many of them were of the incredible vistas, but many were of him as well. He was so touched that Brad had taken the time to take his picture, he was starting to get emotional. When he saw the last photo, he lost it. It was an incredible picture of him and Brad. Their arms were draped over each other's shoulders, and the lake and mountain range were in the background. If you looked closely, you could just make out his plane floating on the lake.

Tears began to roll down his cheeks, and Brad used his thumb to catch them.

"This is the perfect ending to a perfect day, Brad," Mac choked out. "There's only one more thing that could make this day any more perfect."

"What's that?" Brad asked.

"This," Mac said, as he laid Brad down on the couch and ravaged him with kisses.

chapter 24

MAC and Brad made out like high school kids for the longest time.

Mac finally said, "Should we take this to the bed?"

"I thought you'd never ask," Brad said.

They stripped down and climbed into bed and pulled the covers up high. This time, Mac took the lead.

"Brad," Mac whispered. "I want to make some memories right now."

"Then what are you waiting for?"

"I'm not quite sure what to do," Mac said shyly.

"Just do what feels good, and the rest will follow," Brad whispered.

"I've never had a man's dick in my mouth," Mac said. "I'm not sure how or if I can do it. I really want to try, but I don't want to disappoint you."

"Mac, relax," Brad said. "You would never disappoint me. Remember, no expectations."

Mac relaxed a little and melted into Brad. He gently kissed Brad on his lips, then his forehead, then his neck. He passionately caressed Brad's neck and shoulders with his tongue and lips until he could see that Brad had chill bumps all over. He took that as a good sign. He slowly moved down to Brad's huge pectoral muscles. They were hairy, firm, and beautiful, and perfectly framed his big, brown nipples. He gently tugged on Brad's left nipple with his front teeth, and Brad let out a throaty moan. With the nipple erect, Mac pinched it between his thumb and forefinger and twisted a little. That move earned him an arched back and another moan. He did the same to the other, with the same response.

He kissed his way down Brad's taut stomach, following his hairline. Eventually, he reached Brad's pubic hair and inhaled his man scent.

This is hot, he thought. *I've never smelled the intimate scent of another man. What a turn-on.* He continued to take in Brad's scent, but couldn't help noticing the raging hard-on right in front of his very eyes. He closed his eyes and thought, *here goes.*

He took Brad's hard cock into his mouth and went down as far as he could. He stopped when he began to gag. He backed off a little and took some time to get used to it. Brad was rubbing his head encouragingly, which gave him the strength to go on. As he relaxed, so did his throat. He began to move up and down the length of Brad's dick, taking as much as he could without gagging, and found a rhythm. He looked up, and Brad seemed to be enjoying his attempts, which made him feel a little better.

He tried to remember exactly what Brad had done to him the day before that had felt so incredible. He released Brad's dick from his mouth and moved down to his balls. He circled Brad's ball sack with his tongue, savoring the texture and scent. He sucked both balls into his mouth, just as Brad had done, and tossed them gently around in his mouth. Brad planted both feet on the bed beside Mac's head and lifted into the sensation.

Mac was hard as a rock, and his dick needed attention, but it was more important that he continue to pleasure Brad in every way he knew how. He gently released Brad's balls and whispered, "Roll over."

Brad did as he was told and slowly rolled onto his stomach. Mac straddled Brad's ass and saw just how hard his own dick was. He massaged Brad's shoulders and back with gentle but firm strokes, kissing as he went. Mac slid down to Brad's perfect hot ass, which was full and round, and Mac simply studied it while still rubbing Brad's back. He continued to think about what felt good to him and tried to do similar things to Brad.

He slid down even farther until his face was even with Brad's ass. He massaged it with both hands as he kissed his way down his back. He finally got up enough courage to part Brad's ass cheeks and was rewarded with the prettiest, perfectly round pink pucker. He'd never seen a man or woman's butt hole before, and had never even thought what it would look like, but Brad's was beautiful.

He buried his face in Brad's ass and started licking, as Brad had done to him. It wasn't what he expected at all; in fact, it was quite a turn-on. He didn't know what he was expecting, but this wasn't it. The more he did it, the more he enjoyed it. He used his tongue to circle the opening and then forced it in as far as he could. Brad lifted his ass off of the bed and pushed his ass into Mac's face. Mac was even more turned on, and he worked harder to please Brad. He didn't know why, but he wanted Brad's dick in his hand. He reached under Brad and pulled his dick and balls to the back and began to stroke them.

"Oh God, Mac, that feels so good. Please don't stop," Brad asked.

And he didn't. He moistened his finger as Brad had done and slowly pushed it into Brad's hole. It was so tight, he thought he might hurt him, but Brad didn't seem to mind. He worked his finger in and out as Brad moaned and moved under him.

"Mac, fuck me, please?" Brad begged.

"What do I do?" Mac asked.

Brad rolled over and said, "I think I saw a bottle of hand lotion under the sink. That will make things easier."

Mac retrieved the hand lotion and came back to bed.

"I don't have any condoms," Mac said.

"Jeff and I were monogamous, and I haven't been with anyone since he died," Brad said.

"And I haven't been with anyone since Lindsey died, either," Mac said.

"I think we're safe."

Brad positioned himself on his back, looking up at Mac. Mac had a scared look on his face, and Brad stroked his arm to reassure him.

"Remember, you can say stop, and we'll stop," he said.

"Not on your life," Mac said.

Brad instructed Mac to put some lotion on his dick and spread some around his opening. Mac did as instructed and looked down at Brad.

Brad lifted his legs, offering himself up to Mac. Mac positioned his cock at Brad's opening and pushed a little.

"Slowly," Brad said. "It's been a long time."

Mac backed off some. "Tell me when," he said.

"Okay, a little more," Brad instructed.

Mac pushed in a little more and hesitated. Brad nodded, and Mac pushed all the way in and stopped.

"Oh God, Brad, you are so tight. This feels incredible."

"Give me a second," Brad said as he got used to the stretch and the feeling of fullness. "Now move slowly," he said.

Mac began with slow, short strokes. When Brad seemed relaxed and really into it, he picked up the pace. Brad had both hands on Mac's thighs, guiding him along. Mac held Brad's legs over his shoulders while he studied Brad's face. He bent down and kissed Brad passionately over and over as he filled him.

Brad grabbed his dick and began stroking, slowly at first, then picking up the pace.

"I can't last for much longer," Mac whispered. "You are so hot, and I am so close."

"I'm ready, Mac, go for it," Brad said.

Mac picked up the pace until he was pounding Brad's ass into the bed.

Brad closed his eyes and yelled, "I'm going to cum, Mac."

Mac felt Brad's orgasm before he saw it. Brad's ass clamped tightly around Mac's dick as the spurts of cum, one after another, flew out of Brad's cock, landing on his chest and chin.

The sensation was too much for Mac to take. He came just as Brad was emptying his last load.

Brad watched as Mac's head rolled back and he let out this guttural moan and pounded into Brad as hard as he could. When Mac had shot the last of his load into Brad's welcoming gut, he collapsed on top of him.

His dick slipped out of Brad's ass, and he slid to the side, never letting go of his lover. When Mac could speak, he said, "Brad, that was the most intense sex I have ever had. Was I okay? Did it feel okay?"

"You were terrific, Mac. It felt amazing. I never expected to ever have sex with anyone again, not to mention enjoy it so much," Brad said.

Mac smiled because he'd done okay. After all, this was his first time fucking a man.

Brad relaxed when he saw how Mac took a deep breath and seemed to calm down. He even saw what he assumed was a little bit of satisfaction on Mac's face.

Mac looked into Brad's eyes and gently kissed his cheek.

"You are an incredible man, Bradford Mitchell, and that was an incredible experience."

"Mac, I don't know what to say," Brad choked out. "The world works in such mysterious ways. Who would have thought that six months ago, when I showed up at your kiosk looking for a flight to the lodge, that any of this would have ever happened?"

Mac took Brad in his arms and held him tight.

"Whatever or whoever brought us together sure knew we needed each other," Mac whispered. "I've felt emotionally dead since Lindsey died, and you brought me back to life. Thank you."

They stayed in bed the rest of the night, enjoying each other and simply being content.

THE night before Mac was to leave for Anchorage to pick up Zander, Jake, and Jack, they were lying on the couch in front of the fire, sipping brandy. Brad noticed that Mac seemed a bit edgy and a little nervous.

"Is something wrong, Mac? You seem nervous," Brad asked.

"To be truthful, I am a little nervous about Jack's visit," Mac confessed. "I'm not ready to share this thing between us with anyone just yet, especially Lindsey's brother, and I'm not sure I can behave myself."

Brad said, "I'm not sure how to take that, Mac. I can't not be who I am."

Mac held on to Brad a little tighter.

"No, I didn't mean you. I would never ask you to be anything that you're not," he said. "I'm just not ready to get into this with Jack, that's all. I'm living it, and I still don't totally understand it. I can't imagine what Jack is going to think."

"Mac, we can't stay locked away in this cabin the rest of our lives. If this is going to work, we need to be honest with ourselves and the people we love. How do you think my friends are going to react to this? Jeff's been dead just over six months, and I'm already involved with someone else. Hell, it sounds awful hearing the words when I say them, and I think I know how we got here."

"Okay," Mac said. "Why don't we just see how this next week goes and take it from there. How hard can it be to behave ourselves in front of Jack?"

Brad looked up and smiled, and Mac kissed him.

"That's a pretty tall order," Brad said. "But I'll do my best."

"That's all I could ever ask of you, Bradford," Mac said as he buried his face in Brad's neck.

"Let's turn in," Mac said. "We have an early morning."

"Okay by me," Brad said.

They brushed their teeth and slid beneath the warmth of the blankets on their bed. Mac rolled on top of Brad and looked deeply into his eyes with a strange look.

"You have something to say, Mac?" Brad said.

"More like something to ask," Mac replied.

"Go for it," Brad said.

Mac looked a little embarrassed and was starting to blush.

"Come on, Mac," Brad said. "You can ask me anything."

"I want you to do to me what I've been doing to you this entire week," he shyly choked out.

"Mac, you want me to fuck you?" Brad asked, as Mac's face turned a deeper shade of red. "Oh man, why didn't you say so?"

"I didn't know I wanted you to. I mean, I knew it would probably happen sooner or later, but you seem to enjoy it so much, I want to see what it feels like."

"My pleasure," Brad said with a sly grin. "But let me just say, it's not always great the first time. Your body needs time to adjust to the sensation, but I'll be very slow and gentle, and hopefully you'll enjoy it."

Mac slid to Brad's side, and Brad rolled over on top of Mac.

Brad looked down into Mac's eyes. "It's really important to me that you enjoy this, so I'm really going to take my time and get you relaxed and ready."

Mac gave Brad a trusting look and closed his eyes as Brad started nibbling on his earlobe. Brad was rewarded with a shiver, which encouraged him to go further. He kissed his way down to Mac's neck and caressed the same spot that Mac loved so much on him. From there, he slowly licked his way to Mac's left nipple. Mac shivered again as Brad lightly bit down on it and circled his tongue around and around. He slowly moved to Mac's right nipple and flicked his tongue over it until it became as hard as Mac's growing erection.

Brad felt Mac's cock growing against his stomach as he worked his way down Mac's muscular chest and washboard stomach. Mac gasped when Brad encircled his enlarged cock with his warm lips. He held on tight, a handful of bed linens in each hand, as Brad started to move up and down in a slow, steady motion. When Brad thought Mac was getting close to shooting his load, he released his hold on Mac's dick and focused his attention on his balls. He lightly ran his tongue over Mac's scrotum and slowly lifted Mac's legs and pushed them back until Mac's knees were up against his chest.

Finally, he got a glimpse of what he'd been working his way down toward. Mac's pucker was as beautiful and perfect as he remembered. He started by teasing it with the tip of his tongue. Mac's sweet taste had Brad's own cock swelling at an amazing rate. He rubbed his tongue over the sensitive area repeatedly, until he heard Mac begin to purr. He felt Mac's tight hole begin to loosen to his touch as Mac relaxed and went with the feeling. Mac started to squirm under Brad's assault on his ass, moving his hips and thrusting forward into Brad's intrusion. Brad started fucking Mac with his tongue while he pulled Mac's cheeks apart. Brad reached for the lotion on the bedside table and squirted some on his index finger. He rubbed a little on Mac's hole and gently massaged the area. Brad slowly pushed his finger into Mac's tight little ass bit by bit until he was up to the first knuckle. He looked at Mac's face to try and read his expression and was surprised to see a relaxed look and slight smile on Mac's lips. He took this as a sign that he should proceed. He slid his finger farther into Mac's ass until it was in as far as it would go. He lowered his head and again took Mac into his mouth. He slid his mouth all the way down until Mac's dick was resting at the back of his throat. He then turned his finger and found the sweet spot he was looking for.

Mac came up off of the bed as he said, "Oh my God, Brad. What are you doing to me?"

Brad smiled at the question, but he didn't lose his concentration. He continued to move his finger over Mac's prostate while he moved his mouth up and down his huge erection. Mac said, "Brad, I'm so close."

Brad slowly slid his finger out of Mac's ass and released his cock.

"Are you okay, Mac?" he asked.

"Oh yeah," Mac said. "Everything you're doing feels so incredible. I'm so relaxed, I feel like a limp noodle."

Brad scooted up to Mac's ass and squeezed some lotion into his hand and spread it all over himself and again around Mac's waiting hole. He positioned himself against Mac's opening and applied a little pressure. Mac released the bed linens and placed his hand on Brad's thigh, as if to control the intrusion. Brad pushed a little farther until the head of his dick breached Mac's hole.

Mac said, "Wow, give me a minute."

As difficult as it was not to move, Brad stilled himself until Mac gave him the okay. As Mac relaxed and opened up to Brad, he gave him the signal to proceed. Brad slowly applied a little more pressure until Mac finally opened up and accepted him. Brad began to move very slowly. He gently pulled almost all the way out and slowly slid back in. Brad watched the tension leave Mac's body as he gave in to the sensation.

"How are you doing, flyboy?" Brad asked.

"Not bad… such a strange feeling of fullness," he said.

Brad kept moving, very slowly, and finally hit the magic button again. Mac again came off of the bed and said, "There, that feels so good, Brad."

Mac's dick was dripping with precum, and Brad knew he wasn't far from shooting. He reapplied lotion to his hand and began to stroke Mac's dick as he was fucking him.

"Oh Jesus," Mac said.

Brad continued to stroke Mac's cock while Mac guided Brad's dick and controlled the rhythm. Mac pulled Brad up against him as tightly as he could and held him there. "Brad, I'm about to shoot."

He released Brad, and Brad again started to move. Building slowly, he plowed harder and harder into Mac until he felt Mac's ass tighten around his dick. Mac arched his back as Brad continued to stroke Mac's dick through his orgasm. Brad's own balls began to draw up, and he knew he was about to unload into Mac. He felt his own orgasm build as he exploded into Mac.

Mac continued to shoot his load onto his chest as Brad filled his ass. When they were both spent, Brad stopped and held himself tightly against Mac's ass.

Mac lowered his legs and positioned them on both sides of Brad, as Brad withdrew and slid out of him. Mac suddenly felt very empty and wanted Brad back in him, but Brad fell on the bed next to Mac and tried to catch his breath.

Mac was the first one to move. He turned to face Brad and said, "Thank you."

"You're thanking me?" Brad said. "Thank *you*."

Mac smiled and kissed Brad very gently.

"It was amazing and strange all at the same time," Mac said. "That spot you kept rubbing against, man, I thought I was going to crawl out of my skin."

"The amazing prostate," Brad said. "Does it every time."

They laughed for a second, and Mac said, "Seriously, Brad, you are introducing me to so many pleasures I never knew existed. It's like I just crawled out from under a rock."

"Mac, there's so much more I want to show you, and I plan on taking my time doing it," Brad said as he walked to the bathroom to get a wet cloth. He returned and cleaned himself and Mac and dropped the wet towel on the floor. Brad nestled into Mac, and Mac tightened his grip on Brad as they both closed their eyes. Mac felt a sudden flash of fear. *Oh shit, Jack's coming tomorrow*, he thought. *Why do I have this sinking feeling that this little world Brad and I have created for ourselves is about to be blown wide open?*

chapter 25

THE morning came very early. Mac had set the alarm for five o'clock, but he didn't really need it. He hadn't slept for more than two hours off and on and had been up since three o'clock. He kissed Brad's neck as he slid out of bed to get some coffee going. He stood at the foot of the bed, watching Brad sleep.

"We've come so far in six months, Brad," he whispered. "I hope we can hold on to what we have." *I've gone from straight widower to gay lover in just over six months. That must be a record or something*, he thought.

He tiptoed to the kitchen to set up the coffee, naked again—something he'd become very accustomed to in the last week. Something he'd never done before, even when he was alone at home. When the coffee was starting to drip, he headed to the bathroom to take a quick shower and get dressed.

When he came out of the bathroom, Brad was pouring two cups of coffee.

"What are you doing up?" Mac asked.

"I've grown very accustomed to having you in my bed. When you get up, I get up. I've decided I'm taking you down the mountain on the snowmobile."

"Are you now?" Mac asked.

"Yep, it's a beautiful morning, and it's the last bit of time we'll have together for the next week, and I want to enjoy it."

"I'd like that," Mac said.

Brad handed Mac his coffee and kissed him good morning without stopping as he made his way to the bathroom to get showered and dressed.

Mac sat down at the kitchen table with both hands around his warm coffee cup. He bowed his head and looked down into the cup as if searching for an answer. He didn't want Jack to know about him and Brad, not yet, maybe not ever. But he couldn't ask Brad to be anything other than who he was, and he owed it to Brad to not act any differently toward him in front of Jack. So how could they be themselves around Jack and not have Jack pick up on their romantic relationship? He was in a no-win situation, and he couldn't shake this feeling that he was about to lose the only person he'd ever wanted since Lindsey died.

As he was dumping the last of his cold coffee down the drain, Brad stepped out of the bathroom, looking as naturally gorgeous as anyone could look. His wet hair was slicked back, and he was wearing a red plaid flannel shirt and blue jeans. He was simply stunning to look at. *Six months ago, I never even noticed another guy, and now it's all I can do to keep my hands off of him. I've got it bad*, he thought.

He met Brad halfway across the room and took him in his arms. He buried his face in Brad's neck, a spot he realized had become his obsession. He breathed in the familiar scent, mixed with a fresh, soapy smell. He loved to run his tongue over Brad's skin and savor his taste, and he especially loved the way Brad wiggled when he gently nibbled on the sensitive area.

Brad sensed the apprehension in Mac and tried to reassure him the only way he knew how. He held on and melted into his embrace.

Mac looked at his watch and said, "Time to go."

"If you're waiting on me, you're backing up, flyboy," Brad said.

They opened the cabin door to a beautiful, bright, crisp morning. Everything was still white and untouched, with the exception of a few rabbit tracks across the patch.

Brad hopped on the snowmobile with Mac right behind him. Mac wrapped his arms around Brad's waist and hung on tightly. With the push of a button, the engine was whining, and they were gone. Brad took the same route down the mountain they had blazed coming up, and the scenery was just as spectacular. They reached the plane in record time.

"This sure beats hiking," Brad yelled over the whine of the engine.

"No shit, huh?" Mac replied.

Brad pulled up to the little dock and turned off the engine. He sat on the snowmobile and watched Mac as he climbed into the plane and started the engine while he did his checklist.

Brad could see the hesitation in Mac's step, something he had never witnessed before, as Mac was always so self-assured. Mac was in distress, and he felt for him, but sooner or later, if this relationship was going to work, Mac needed to come clean to his brother-in-law and daughter. But Brad decided that he would make it as easy on Mac as he could. He would try to not do anything to clue Jack in on their relationship until Mac was ready—if he would ever be ready. He would follow Mac's lead when it came to Jack.

When the checklist was finished, Mac joined Brad at the snowmobile.

Brad was humming a song he hadn't thought about since his parents died.

"That about does it," Mac said. "What's that you're humming?"

"Before I share that, can we talk for a minute before you take off?" Brad asked.

"Sure," Mac said.

Brad looked off into the distance and took in the full beauty of his surroundings. "I know you're struggling, Mac. I can see it in your every move. And I don't know what I can do about it."

Mac turned Brad's face toward his and said, "Look at me, Brad. I can't ask you to do anything about it. It wouldn't be fair to you, and being fair to you is really important to me. I promised you that I would never ask you to be anyone but yourself, and I'll keep that promise. I—"

Brad interrupted as he turned his head away again. "I know right now that you would like nothing better than for the two of us to spend the rest of our lives tucked away in our little paradise, but that's not reality, Mac. There's a huge world out there, and now that I have a second chance at happiness, I feel like I want to experience it all... with you."

Mac looked out to where Brad was staring.

Still staring in the distance, Brad said, "The song I was humming is a song that was sung at my parents' funeral. It's called 'I'm Gonna Live Till I Die', and they did. I hadn't thought about that song in so many years, but sitting here, watching you prepare to leave, brought them back to me. The words say a lot about how I'm feeling right now."

Brad started to sing the song. "'Ain't gonna miss a thing, I'm gonna have my fling. I'm gonna live, live, live till I die.'"

Brad stopped singing and finally turned to look Mac in the eyes. Tears were running down his cheeks, and Mac was heartbroken. He reached up and brushed the tears away with his thumb, and Brad took his hand in his.

"When I walked into that airport," he said. "I was emotionally dead. I was simply going through the motions of life, and you pulled me through. And now, because of you, I want it all. I want you, Mac, and I want to live because of you."

Now tears were falling down Mac's cheeks as well, and it was Brad's turn to wipe them away.

Brad continued. "Mac, I will be on my best behavior. You mean too much to me to lose you now. I won't do anything to jeopardize your relationship with Jack, or Zoe-Grace, for that matter. What and when you tell them will be your decision."

Mac launched toward Brad so hard they both fell off the other side of the snowmobile into a pile of snow.

"Thank you, Brad," he said. "I just need a little time to adjust, and I will tell them, I promise you."

Brad put his arms around Mac's neck and kissed him.

"Hurry back, flyboy," he said. "I'll be waiting."

Mac nodded and stood. He helped Brad to his feet, and together, hand in hand, they walked to the plane. Mac climbed into the cockpit while Brad released the lines. Mac waved as Brad watched the little plane holding his future take to the sky. He watched until the plane was out of sight. He decided to hike back up the mountain and leave the snowmobile for Mac and Jack when they returned.

chapter 26 ✈

BRAD got back to the cabin after a breathtaking hike and immediately turned on the VHF radio. Eventually, he heard a static-fused Mac request permission to land, and knew Mac had made it safely to Anchorage. He was carrying in the last load of firewood as he again heard Mac's familiar voice requesting permission to take off.

Well, he thought. *They'll be here in an hour or so, and this should be very interesting.*

Brad continued to do chores around the cabin to busy himself until they arrived. He was on his hands and knees, scrubbing the shower, when he heard, "November 4649 Delta calling Wing Mansion, Wing Mansion, do you copy?"

Brad dropped the sponge and ran for the radio.

"This is Wing Mansion. Over."

"Hey, Brad, switch to channel one eight. Over."

"Wing Mansion switching to one eight."

"Wing Mansion to November 4649 Delta. Over."

"Hey, Brad, how's it going? Over."

"It's going great here. Did you pick up your passengers? Over."

"All three are on board and whiny as hell. They keep asking for peanuts. Over."

"Don't they know that no reputable airline will serve peanuts anymore? Over."

"I don't think they saw the memo. Brad, once we land, I'll walk over to the lodge and get another snowmobile, and we'll see you shortly. Over."

"No need, Mac, I hiked up so you boys could have the snowmobile. I knew you'd have luggage. Over."

"Good man. Over."

"Yeah, I know. What's your ETA, Mac? Over."

"We'll be on the ground in about twenty, so we'll see you in just under an hour. Over."

Knowing Mac had headphones on and the passengers couldn't hear him, he said, "Be careful, Mac. Over."

"Roger that, see you in a little while. Over. November 4649 Delta switching back to channel one six."

"Wing Mansion standing by on channel one six."

Brad went back and finished cleaning the bathroom, made the bed, and straightened up a little. *We're a couple of slobs*, he thought as he picked up a pair of Mac's dirty underwear lying next to the bed. He didn't want to be gross, but he sat on the side of the bed and put the underwear up to his nose. The richness of Mac's sweet man scent immediately filled his nostrils. His senses kicked in, and he began to get an erection. He quickly stood and deposited the dirty underwear in the clothes hamper before he got himself in trouble. He picked up a book and headed for the porch to wait for the boys.

Right on schedule, he heard the whine of the snowmobile making its way up the mountain. If Mac was anything, he was prompt, and Brad loved that about him. When the snowmobile pulled up to the porch, Brad stood to greet them. Jack was the first one to hop off. He walked up to the porch to greet Brad.

"Hey, Brad, how's it going?" Jack asked.

"Very well, thanks," Brad responded. "How was the flight?"

"Besides the cheap pilot not offering any snacks, I guess it was okay." Jack chuckled.

Mac climbed the four stairs to the porch and slapped Brad on the arm.

"Passengers these days, you just can't please them. Especially when they pay the cheap fare, cheap as in *free!*" Mac shouted over his shoulder as he walked into the cabin.

"Let me grab your bag," Brad said.

"Wow, the maid must have come," Mac yelled from inside the cabin.

"Yep, she just left, so you better keep the place up, or you're paying her next time," Brad replied.

"Jack, come in and let me show you around," Brad continued.

Walking through the door and looking around, Jack said, "Wow, this place is perfect."

"Jack, do you remember when I first rented that plane and started flying for the lodge?"

"Sure, Lindsey used to talk about it all the time," Jack replied.

"Well, sometimes we would come up for the weekend and hike these trails. And believe it or not, this is the same cabin we used to dream about owning. Of course back then, this place was rundown and very basic, but it didn't matter, because we couldn't afford it anyway." Mac continued. "When Brad told me he was buying a cabin, I had no idea it was one and the same. But the moment I saw it, I knew this was it, and I said yes immediately."

"I'm happy for you, man," Jack said. "And you too, Brad."

"Thanks," Brad said. "Did Zander and Jake have a good vacation?"

"They said they did," Mac said. "Oh, and by the way, I hope you don't mind, but I invited them up for dinner. I thought we would just throw some steaks on the fire and have a little vino."

"Sounds like fun," Brad said.

"Great," Mac said. "Oh and Jack, you can have the loft, and I'll bunk in with Brad."

Jack said, "Are you sure? I don't want to put you out of your bed. I can certainly sleep on the couch."

"We won't hear of it," Mac said. "And besides, it's easier to manage the fire from down here. Remember, it's the only heat source we have, and this little place can get quite cold at night."

Jack looked at Mac with a puzzled expression on his face, then said, "As long as I'm not putting anyone out."

"Good, it's settled then," Brad said.

Once Jack was settled in the loft, he said, "I think I'll take a walk outside and see what I can see. Do you mind?"

"Help yourself," Mac and Brad said simultaneously.

When Mac was sure Jack was far enough from the cabin and exploring, he grabbed Brad and gave him a big kiss.

"Careful, Mac, Jack might see us," Brad said.

"He's outside. And besides, we get to sleep together," Mac whispered.

"That was a smooth move, Mac. Now all I have to do is figure out a way to keep my hands off of you."

"Don't try too hard," Mac said. "I don't think Jack can see through blankets."

"Lucky for us," Brad said.

"I think this will work out just fine. I can't thank you enough, Brad, for doing this for me."

"You're welcome. Now get outside and find your brother-in-law."

Mac stole another quick kiss and skipped out like a giddy Cub Scout.

He searched the grounds until he found Jack sitting on a rock, looking at the view.

"It sure is beautiful up here. I can see why you and Lindsey loved it so much," Jack said.

Jack moved over a little, and Mac sat down next to him. "I never get tired of looking at this view," Mac said.

"I know what you mean, man. I wouldn't either," Jack continued. "You and Brad seem to be okay."

"Yeah, he's a great guy. We get along really well and have a lot in common. I was so lucky that he invited me to buy this place with him."

"What does Zoe-Grace think of the place?" Jack asked.

"She's not been up yet. She doesn't have any time off until Christmas. That girl is taking so many classes; I don't know how she does it. Her biological parents must have been really smart. Lindsey and I barely made it through college with a two-point-five grade point average." Mac laughed. "I'm so proud of her."

"Lindsey would be too," Jack said.

"I know," Mac said. "I wish she were here to see all of this."

They both stood and walked back toward the cabin. They heard the whining of the snowmobiles before they saw them and knew it must be Zander and Jake.

They picked up their pace to meet them at the front of the cabin.

"Hey, guys," Mac shouted as they pulled up the trail.

Brad heard their arrival and also came out to greet them. They all exchanged hellos and settled down on the porch to have a beer and hear all about Zander and Jake's travels. The guys talked until it was time to start dinner. Mac put the potatoes in the hot coals and put the steaks on the grill in the fireplace while Brad tossed a salad and opened wine.

Before long, they were all chomping on steaks and baked potatoes and enjoying each other's company. When everyone was full and the dishes were done, they retired to the living room. Zander and Jake made their good-byes, as they wanted to make it down the mountain before dark.

Jack and Brad sat on the couch while Mac took the chair, and they all had their shoes off and feet up on the old coffee table. In the background, Dinah Washington was singing "September in the Rain," and all seemed okay. Mac took one look around the cabin and thought he worried way too much. He owed Brad big time, and he thought he would have lots of time to thank him properly.

After another brandy, Jack said, "I'm beat, guys. I hope you don't mind, but I'm going to brush my teeth and turn in."

"Of course we don't," Mac said as Brad nodded.

When Jack came out of the bathroom, he shook Brad's hand, and Mac stood and they hugged.

"Good night, guys," Jack said.

Jack climb the ladder to the loft, and when Mac saw the oil lamp go out, he whispered, "You ready to turn in?"

Brad stood and picked up the brandy glasses and put them in the sink. They took turns in the bathroom, and within minutes they were under the covers with nothing but the firelight to illuminate the cabin.

Mac took Brad in his arms and whispered, "I missed you today."

"What do you mean, missed me? We were together most of the day," Brad whispered back.

"Yeah, we were together, but we weren't really together, if you get my drift."

"I get your drift, but it's going to be that way for a few more days, so you better get used to it," Brad whispered.

"Don't remind me," Mac said in a low, sexy voice.

Mac quietly kissed Brad and made his signature move right to Brad's neck. He nibbled at his favorite spot until Brad was squirming around like a snake. Mac reached down and took Brad's dick into his hands and began to stroke.

"Mac, are you sure this is wise?" Brad asked in a very low voice.

"As long as we're quiet, he won't hear a thing," Mac said.

"You don't have to tell me twice," Brad whispered as he grabbed Mac's already rock-hard dick and began to move his hand up and down. When he heard Mac's slow, soft moans, he knew he was on the right track. Mac pulled the covers over their heads and dove in to the ecstasy that awaited them.

Since the covers were over their heads, neither of them saw the pair of eyes looking down at them from the tiny loft.

chapter 27

MAC slowly opened his eyes. He was snuggled in against Brad's back with his arms tightly wrapped around him and his head resting in—where else?—the crook of Brad's neck. He glanced at the clock and saw that it was six fifty. He slowly tried to slide away from Brad without waking him, but as soon as he moved, Brad pulled him in tighter.

"Good morning," he whispered. "If you let me up, I'll make the coffee."

"Noooooo," Brad whined. "Can't you make it from here?"

"Trust me, I wish I could," he responded.

"This is the last time I'll forget to set the auto brew," Brad said in a hushed tone.

"Yeah, so it's your fault I have to get out of this warm bed," Mac said.

"Oh, quit whining and hurry back," Brad said as he rolled over and pulled the covers over his head.

With Brad no longer against him, Mac rolled over, pulled back the covers, and put his feet on the floor. Something caught his eye, and he glanced in the direction of the movement. Jack was sitting on the couch, looking straight ahead. He was fully dressed, and his bag was next to him.

Mac quickly realized that Jack must have come down from the loft at God knows what time and saw him and Brad in bed cuddled up and very cozy.

"Shit," he said under his breath. He looked down and tried to compose himself before he attempted to speak.

Panic overtook him for a moment. He forced himself to calm down, took a deep breath, and stood, trying to look as calm as he could.

"Jack," he squeaked. "What are you doing up so early?"

Jack didn't answer him.

"Jack?" he said again, a little louder this time.

Jack turned his head and glared at Mac.

"So you're a queer now?" Jack said in a monotone voice.

Mac stood silently, looking at Jack.

"Holy shit," Brad said from under the covers when he heard Jack's comment. "This isn't good."

He started to get up and join Mac, but immediately stopped when he heard Mac's response.

Taken back by Jack's bluntness and unsure of how to answer the question, Mac went into survival mode. "Hell no," he said. "What are you talking about?"

"You two were very cozy in bed this morning!" Jack shouted. "Not to mention what I saw last night," he added, as he stood and paced in front of the couch.

"Oh God," Jack said. "My best friend and dead sister's husband is a queer."

Mac walked toward him. "Jack, wait, let me explain," he shouted.

"Don't come near me," Jack roared. "What's to explain? Did you fuck guys when Lindsey was alive? And Zoe-Grace, what will she think? Did you think of the consequences before you jumped into bed with him?" he asked, as he gestured toward the bed.

Before Mac could speak, Brad hopped out of bed and stood behind him.

"Mac," Brad whispered. "What do you want me to do?"

Mac turned to look at Brad and saw the disillusionment in his eyes, but he knew Brad was there to support him, even if Brad was disappointed in him.

"Just give me some time to explain all of this to Jack," Mac said. "Things will be okay."

"Why don't you and your boyfriend here go back to bed?" Jack said. "I'm leaving anyway. I don't want to disrupt your little love den. No wonder you were so hell-bent on buying this place with him."

"Jack, wait," Mac pleaded.

"Mac, I'm leaving, one way or the other. If you won't fly me back to Anchorage, I'll charter a plane to come and get me. The choice is yours. But while you're deciding, here's one more choice you need to make. If you don't come home with me and leave your little fairy loverboy behind, you can kiss this friendship good-bye."

Brad waited for a second to see if Mac was going to allow Jack to refer to him as a "fairy loverboy," but Mac simply stood there, mouth open with that "deer in the headlights" look Brad had seen before.

Brad had had enough. He stepped around Mac and rushed across the room, cocking his fist in midair. The blow landed hard on Jack's jaw. Jack stumbled back, caught his balance, and swung in Brad's direction, but missed him by a foot. Brad took the opportunity to strike Jack again, this time knocking him to the ground. He brushed his hands together like he had just taken out the trash and said, "That's a little something to take back to Anchorage from the fairy lover boy." He glared at Mac as he walked by him and went into the bathroom.

Mac, stunned, rushed to Jack and helped him up. He sat Jack on the couch while he ran to the kitchen to get something to help with the bleeding. Jack's lip was split open, and his eye was already starting to turn purple. When Mac returned, he knelt in front of Jack and put the wet cloth on his bleeding lip.

"Jack, please just let me explain."

"The only thing I want to know from you is if you're taking me back to Anchorage," Jack mumbled with the cloth tightly pushed up against his lip. "It's him or your family."

Defeated, Mac said, "Let me get dressed."

Brad came out of the bathroom, and as he walked past Jack sitting on the couch, he said with a grin, "How was that for a fairy loverboy ass-whipping, Mr. Macho Straight Man?"

Jack looked up and glared at him. "You caught me off guard. You won't be so lucky next time," he said with a sneer.

Brad opened his mouth to speak, and Mac held his hand and said, "Enough, Brad."

"So, Mac, what are you going to do?" Brad asked. "You sending his ass packing, or are you going with him?"

Mac looked at Jack with a pleading look. Jack turned his head in the other direction.

"Jack, can you give us a second?" Mac asked.

Jack, looking pretty ill and very disgusted, stood and walked out to the porch.

"Mac, I told you this day would come," Brad said. "It came way sooner than either one of us imagined, but it came just the same. And what you do right now will affect the rest of your life *and* my life."

"Brad, I've got to fly him home. He won't be able to get another pilot to come and get him on such short notice, and it's obvious he won't stay here. What can I do?" Mac asked.

"The way I see it, the one thing Jack is right about is your two choices," Brad said. "I would prefer that you let the asshole fend for himself. Hell, I'll even pay to put him up at the lodge until he can get a flight back. But if you choose to go, you shouldn't come back."

"Brad, you can't be serious?"

"I'm very serious, Mac. This is the time in one's life when you stand up for what's right or turn and run, with your tail between your legs. And from the look on your face, I can see that your tail is tucked and ready to go."

"Brad, it's not that simple," Mac pleaded.

"Oh, but it is," he shot back. "It's him or me, Mac, very simple choice. And right now, in this very second, I don't care who you choose."

"Brad, you're pissed, and you have a right to be, but you can't mean that," Mac said.

"I'm such a stupid fool," Brad whispered. "I knew I was holding on to some fantasy world, believing that when push came to shove, you'd choose me."

"Brad," Mac pleaded.

"Just stop, Mac," Brad said. "Jeff was the only man I could ever count on, and I was so naïve to think that there would be anyone else. You've obviously made your decision, so please go."

Mac listened with teary eyes as Brad's words cut right through to his heart. He had brought Brad back to life and nurtured him into a sense of security that wasn't real. How could he have done that? He had really thought he loved Brad, but he couldn't commit to this lifestyle. He couldn't disappoint Jack. He and Jack were brothers in every sense of the word. Jack was Zoe-Grace's only uncle, and he couldn't take that away from her. And Zoe-Grace—how would she handle this? He just couldn't disrupt what little family he had left, no matter how he felt about Brad. His decision was made.

Mac turned away from Brad and took his clothes into the bathroom. Brad went to the kitchen and started making coffee.

I'm gonna need a lot of this today, Brad thought.

When Mac came out of the bathroom, he was dressed and carrying his toiletries bag. He climbed the ladder to the loft, packed what few clothes he'd brought, and threw the bag over the rail. He climbed back down and walked into the kitchen.

"I'm so sorry, Brad," he whispered.

"I'm the sorry one," Brad said. "I'll get all your tools down to the lodge, and you can pick them up there. I'll have my bank send you a check to cover your half of the investment, and it will all be over, just as quickly as it started."

Mac reached out to touch Brad, but Brad pulled away.

"Mac, I'm not trying to be dramatic. I'm doing everything I can to keep it together right now, and the slightest touch from you will send everything tumbling down around me. I can't have that be your last thought of me, and I won't give Jack the satisfaction. Now just please go, I'm begging you."

Mac turned around, picked up his bag, and walked out of the door. Brad shakily slid down into a kitchen chair. He folded both of his arms on the table, laid his head in his arms, and silently started to weep.

MAC hopped on the snowmobile with Jack behind him and took off at record-breaking speed. When he got down the mountain, he dropped Jack off at the plane and took the snowmobile to the lodge. After stowing the vehicle away, he walked inside and found Jake.

"Jake, this thing with Brad and me sharing the cabin isn't going to work," he explained. "I'm going back to Anchorage and, unfortunately, I have to resign as your lodge pilot."

"What are you talking about, Mac?" Jake said. "You've been with us since, well, almost the beginning."

"I know, and I've enjoyed every minute of it, and I'm sorry," Mac said as he hung his head. "When I get to Anchorage, I'll make a few calls and see if I can hook you up with another pilot."

"Damn it, Mac," Jake shouted. "We don't want another pilot. What in the hell is going on with you and Brad? Zander and I picked up on something last night. Excuse me if I'm crossing the line here, but are you two romantically involved?"

Mac looked up with tears in his eyes. "I've got to go, Jake. Jack is waiting at the plane, and besides, I'm sure Brad will fill you in. But please do me a favor and check on him. He's a great guy, and he's going to need you and Zander for a while. He's not even over losing Jeff and now this."

Jake nodded, and Mac quickly turned away and rushed out of the door.

Brad watched the little floatplane take off and fly away until it was totally out of sight. He went to the kitchen, poured himself another cup of coffee, and this time added a shot of brandy. He walked back out to the porch and sat in his normal chair. He glanced at Mac's empty chair beside him, and totally lost it. He cried for Jeff, he cried for Mac, but mostly, he cried for himself. When he had no more tears, he walked inside to wash his face and heard a familiar voice.

"Lake Hood Tower, this is November 4649 Delta requesting permission to land. Over."

Brad walked over to the VHF radio and turned it off.

chapter 28

THE flight back to Anchorage was silent except for the chatter of the radio. There was another storm moving in the next day, and reports were being transmitted every fifteen minutes. Mac spent the entire flight thinking and worrying about Brad being alone at the cabin for another storm.

Once they'd landed and taxied over to the dock, Mac brought the plane to a stop. He shut off the engine and turned to Jack.

"Now, can I explain?" he asked.

"Mac, please, I don't want to hear it. I just want to pretend this whole thing never happened. I don't ever want to discuss it or Brad Mitchell ever again. Okay?"

Mac hung his head, crawled out of the pilot's seat, and exited the plane. After removing their bags, he secured the plane, and he and Jack walked silently to his kiosk. As promised, he made a few calls and put the word out that Zander and Jake would be looking for a new pilot, but Christmas was a couple of weeks away, and he knew it would be difficult to find someone until the first of the year.

"Mac, what are your plans for Christmas?" Jack asked in a very cold tone.

"I don't really have any," Mac said. "Zoe-Grace is coming home for Christmas break at the end of the week, and I guess the three of us will do what we always do, unless you have other plans?"

"No other plans," Jack said. "I'll call you in a couple of days. Later."

Instead of the usual hug they always exchanged when they said good-bye, Jack turned and walked away. Shocked at the change in Jack's demeanor, Mac was suddenly full of resentment. Jack had made him choose between family and his first chance at happiness since Lindsey died, and now was treating him like a stranger. In that second, he also realized that he was nothing more than a coward who didn't stand up for someone who loved him and, more importantly, whom he loved. Brad would never forgive him, and how could he ever ask him to? He watched Jack smugly walk toward his car, as he stood beside his empty truck. *I should have beaten the shit out of the guy myself. The hell with him*, he thought.

I'll fly back to the lake and make this right. But how can I show up there after what I've done to Brad? And even if I could muster up the courage to show my face, I don't think that Brad even wants me anymore.

He climbed into his truck and rested his arms and head on the steering wheel as the tears flowed freely. When he composed himself, he started the engine and pulled out of the parking lot.

WHEN Mac got home, there was a strange car in the driveway. He parked his truck on the street, grabbed his bag out of the back, and walked up the sidewalk. He put his key in the door, but before he could unlock it, the door flew open and Zoe-Grace jumped into his arms.

"Daddy!" she screamed as she held on tightly.

"Zoe?" He swung her around and said, "What are you doing here? You weren't due home for another week."

"The semester finished up a little early, and I wanted to surprise you," she said.

Mac's eyes again filled with tears, and he couldn't help himself. He started sobbing on her shoulder.

"Daddy, what's wrong?"

"Nothing, honey," he said. "I'm just so happy to see you."

Zoe-Grace stepped back and looked Mac in the eyes. "What are you not telling me?" she asked.

Mac noticed a young man standing in the doorway, observing the reunion.

"Nothing," he said. "Who do we have here?"

"Dad, I want you to meet Zachary Williams. Zach, meet my dad, McGovern Cleary."

The two men shook hands.

"Nice to meet you, Zach," Mac said.

"Same here, Mr. Cleary."

"My friends call me Mac."

Zoe jumped in, saying, "Daddy, I hope you don't mind that I brought Zach home for the holidays."

"Of course not, the more the merrier," he replied.

"He has to leave on Christmas Eve, as he has to see his parents, but he can stay until then. Is that okay?"

"Sure it is," Mac said. "He can stay as long as he likes. Let's take this inside," he continued. "No need giving the neighbors more of a show than we need to."

Once inside, they made their way to the den and sat down. Mac sat in his favorite chair and Zoe-Grace sat next to Zach on the sofa.

"I still can't believe you're here," Mac said. "I apologize about the condition of the house. I've been at the lake for the last week. In fact, I wasn't planning on coming home until next week, so I'm glad plans changed, or you and Zach would have been here alone."

"I'm glad too, and by the way, everything looks fine. How is the cabin?"

"Not too good, honey," Mac said. "But I'll fill you in later."

"And Brad?" she asked.

"About the same," Mac said.

Zoe frowned, but said, "Okay."

Mac looked at his daughter, and she seemed to be glowing.

"Wow, you look great, honey," Mac said.

"Thanks, Dad," Zoe said as she nervously entwined her fingers in Zach's.

Mac watched closely as the young couple beamed at each other. Mac couldn't help but envy what appeared to be two very happy people.

"Dad, we have some news," Zoe said.

Mac's heart stopped. He sensed what was coming next, but he did his best to hold on to his composure.

"Dad, Zach asked me to marry him last night, and I said yes," she explained.

"What? How long have you two known each other?" Mac asked.

"A couple of years, Mr. Clear... I mean, Mac," Zach said. "We dated casually during part of that time, but neither of us was ready to get too serious. About six months ago, we ended up in a class together, and the rest is history."

"Dad, I wanted to tell you about Zach, but we kept playing phone tag, and I didn't want to tell you over voicemail."

Frozen in his seat, Mac looked at Zoe. His little girl was getting married.

"Mac, I know this probably sounds sudden to you, but I love Zoe very much, and she loves me, and if you think about it, it really isn't that sudden."

"It seems sudden enough to me. Are you sure about all of this?" Mac asked.

"Yes, sir, we're sure," Zach said.

"Dad, we're about to start our first year of residency. I think we're old enough to know when it's right."

"You're right, honey." Mac stood. "Come over here and give your old man a hug," he said.

Zoe crawled into her father's embrace and hugged him tightly around the neck. Zach stood and walked over to where the two were standing. Zoe released her father, and Mac shook Zach's hand. "Welcome to the family," he said as he eyed the young man. "You and I can talk later. Right now, we need to celebrate. Zoe, have you told your Uncle Jack yet?"

"Not yet, I wanted to tell you first," she said.

"Why don't you call him, while Zach and I open some bubbly?" Mac said.

Zoe ran for the phone while Zach and Mac walked to the kitchen to see if he had some champagne in the fridge.

"So, Zach, are your parents happy?" Mac asked. "I assume you told them while you were there last weekend," he added.

"Yes, sir, they love Zoe, and they are very happy for us," Zach said.

Zoe came back into the kitchen as Mac was popping the cork.

"Uncle Jack didn't answer, so I left him a message to call me," she explained.

Mac poured the champagne, and they toasted to a long, successful marriage.

"So when is this event going to take place?" Mac asked.

"We're thinking about July of next year," Zoe said. "And Dad, we think we'd like to get married up at the lake. I know how much Mom loved it there, and it would make me feel like she was there. Do you think Zander and Jake would let us take over the lodge and make a destination wedding out of it?"

Mac panicked as the events of the day came rushing back to him. He tried to look calm and said, "I don't see why not."

"So it's all right with you?" she asked.

"Whatever you want, honey, is fine with me," he replied.

Mac and Zach spent the rest of the day getting acquainted, while Zoe-Grace rummaged through the pantry, trying to find something she could put together for dinner. After they'd eaten pasta primavera and watched a little television, Zach excused himself and went to bed.

Zoe again sat in her father's lap.

"Dad, please tell me what's wrong," she asked. "You've not been yourself since we arrived, and I know you're trying to be happy for us, but something's really bothering you."

Not able to contain himself, Mac started to cry. He held on to Zoe and sobbed for the second time today. Zoe held him and rubbed his back as he cried.

"Daddy, please tell me what's wrong. You know you can tell me anything, right?" she whispered. Mac tried to compose himself.

"Does this have anything to do with the cabin or Brad?" she asked.

"Zoe, a great deal has happened in the last six months that I need to tell you about," Mac said.

Zoe looked a little confused. "Okay, Dad."

Mac took a deep breath and said, "Zoe, you know I love you and you are the most important thing to me, right?"

"Of course I know that. Daddy, now you're starting to scare me."

Mac opened up to Zoe and told her how he and Brad had met. How they reconnected. How Brad lost Jeff. How they fell in love. And... finally, how he'd screwed it all up.

Zoe got out of Mac's lap and started to pace in front of the fireplace.

"You and Brad?" she asked.

Mac nodded. "Honey, we didn't plan on it. In fact, it was the last thing on either of our minds. I'm not gay, and Brad was devastated after losing Jeff."

"Obviously you *are* gay, Dad, or at least bisexual. Did Mom know?"

"Of course not. Hell, I didn't even know. I've never been attracted to another man. In fact, I've never even looked at another person except your mother, until now."

"And how does all this make you feel, Daddy?"

"Confused and scared," he confessed. "But more importantly, how does this make you feel?"

"I don't know how I feel. I guess I'm still in shock," she confessed. "It's strange to think of you one way all my life, and then suddenly think of you another way. I guess I just need a little time to process all this."

"I know what you mean," Mac said. "But I guess it really doesn't matter now anyway. I let Brad down, and he'll probably never forgive me. And besides, I have no interest in anyone else, male or female."

"But, Dad," Zoe said, "just because I need time to process this, doesn't mean I have a problem with it. I have lots of gay friends, and... I promised Zach that I wouldn't spring this on you, but my future in-laws are gay."

"Are you serious?" Mac asked.

"Yep," Zoe said. "Zach is adopted, like me, and his dads are gay. They live in Seattle."

"No shit," Mac said. "And you're okay with that?"

"Sure," she said. "They are the nicest, most normal guys you'll ever meet. I spent last weekend with them, and we all had a blast. I love them and I'd be a hypocrite if I turned my back on you just because you found happiness with a man, gay or not."

Mac stood and sat on the hearth next to Zoe. He put his arm around her and said, "I hope you know how much I love you."

"Dad, Mom and I always knew that you loved us, and when Mom was dying, she made you promise to move on with your life and be happy. I'm not sure this is what she had in mind, but happiness comes in many forms. What makes you think she wouldn't want to see you in love again?" she asked.

"Your Uncle Jack said—"

Zoe interrupted him. "When have you started listening to Uncle Jack? Does his life seem that perfect to you? No, it's a mess. Married, divorced, and he can't seem to find a lasting relationship. Why would you take romantic advice from him? If you ask me, I think you were scared, and you used Uncle Jack as a scapegoat. Heck, at one point I even thought *he* might be gay, and I'm not quite convinced he's not."

"Jack gay?" Mac asked. "But how do you explain his homophobic reaction to Brad and me?"

"Many guys who are in the closet appear homophobic to keep their cover, but Dad, this isn't about Uncle Jack. This is about you and Brad."

Mac thought about that for a minute, and she did have a point, about everything.

"You must get your wisdom from your mother. I don't know how I ever got through a day without you two helping me along," Mac said. "But all this is a moot point, because there is no Brad and me. I really just needed to be honest with you."

"I'm not so sure, Dad. Go to him, tell him how you feel," Zoe advised.

Mac didn't say anything for a few minutes while he thought this through. "But what if he doesn't want me? What if I messed things up too badly?"

"Then at least you'll know," she said.

"You're right. I've got to try and fix this. I'll check the weather and see if I can fly up first thing in the morning, before the storm hits. Will you and Zach be here for a few days? I promise to be back before Christmas, and if this works out, do you mind if I bring Brad back with me?" Mac asked with a new excitement in his voice.

"I don't mind at all, and don't worry about Zach and me, we'll be fine," she said. "Go and get Brad."

Mac looked Zoe in the eyes. "I love you, Zoe-Grace Cleary."

"I love you too, Daddy."

Mac went to his bedroom. He undressed and crawled into bed. He laid his head on his pillow and thought of Brad. *He must be so alone and hurt, and it's all because of me. I've got to make it up to the lake tomorrow before the storm. I just have to.*

chapter 29 ✈

BRAD had passed out on the couch after several glasses of brandy, and woke with a horrible headache. He rummaged around in his medical bag until he found some aspirin, popped a few, and then downed a glass of water. It was three o'clock in the afternoon when he heard a knock at the door.

He ran for the door, half-expecting to see Mac standing there, but was disappointed when it was Zander and Jake.

"Hey, guys," Brad said. "Come in."

Zander jumped right in. "Brad, please tell us what's going on between you and Mac," he said.

"What did Mac tell you?" Brad asked.

"All he said was that it didn't work out between you two, and that he had to resign, and we needed to find another pilot," Jake said. "Oh, and he asked us to check on you."

"Really," Brad said. "That was so nice of him. Look, guys, I consider you both very good friends, and I'm really sorry about his resigning, but I didn't ask him to do that."

"We consider both of you good friends as well, and it doesn't really matter whose decision it was to resign, but we would really like to know why and what's going on," Zander said.

"Since Mac asked you to check on me, then he involved you in this saga, so I guess you have a right to know."

They all sat down, and Brad filled them in on the entire story, from the great beginning to the horrible ending. When he was finished explaining the story, the cabin was silent. Brad wiped a lone tear from his cheek and pulled his knees up against his chest and shivered. Zander was the first to speak.

"Jake and I picked up on something between you guys last night, but we had no idea it had gotten so serious," he said.

"I think it snuck up on us as well," Brad said. "The last thing I was looking for when I landed up here was a relationship, especially one with a straight man. But this thing came out of nowhere, and I don't think either of us saw it coming. We both fought it, and we both struggled with it, until we finally gave in. In hindsight, I should have packed my bags and hightailed it out of Dodge the first time he kissed me."

"Maybe Mac just needs some time," Jake said.

"I don't know," Brad said. "I said some pretty harsh things to him when he left. I told him if he chose to leave with Jack, that he shouldn't come back. Did I mention that I beat the shit out of Jack?" Brad asked.

"Really?" Zander and Jake said simultaneously.

"Yep, he called me a fairy loverboy, so I knocked the hell out of him. He swung at me and missed, and I flattened him. Damn, it felt good. So now you know the story."

"Wow, if I didn't know you guys, I would swear that this was a soap opera," Zander said.

"Yeah, well, it's over now, so no more drama," Brad said.

"On another note," Zander said. "Are you prepared for tomorrow's storm? It's supposed to be pretty bad—six feet of snow and sixty-knot winds."

"I'm all set," Brad said. "The solar panels are still secured from the last storm, and all I need to do is close and lock the shutters. I've got plenty of firewood, food, and brandy. I also heard the weather report a little while ago, and it doesn't sound too good."

"Would you like to come down to the lodge and ride it out with us?" Zander asked.

"Nah, I appreciate the offer, but I need to decide what I'm going to do with my life, and this is the perfect time to do it. No distractions."

"Do you want us to keep our VHF radio on?" Jake asked.

"I'll be fine, don't worry about it," Brad said. "Mac and I passed the last storm here, and it was pretty uneventful."

"I tell you what, we'll leave our radio on if you do. Just in case we may need each other, but remember, being down at the lake, we don't get as good a reception as you do up here," Zander said.

"I'll remember that, and thanks for checking up on me, guys. You're great friends," Brad said.

Zander and Jake stood to leave. "We better get going; we still have some things to do around the lodge before tomorrow morning."

"Be careful heading down the mountain," Brad said. "And if you need me for anything, remember I'll have my radio on," he said as he closed the door.

The cabin was again empty and quiet. Brad started a fire and lit his oil lamps. He walked to his bed, the bed he and Mac had shared for the last week. He lay on Mac's side and wrapped his arms around Mac's pillow. He took a deep breath and inhaled Mac's scent. He buried his face in the pillow and silently cried. *It is going to be a long winter*, he thought.

chapter 30

MAC got out of bed at four thirty, without much sleep. He checked his weather radio, and the storm was due to arrive at the mountain range by late morning, which meant that if he left at first light, he could make it to the lake before the worst of it hit.

He dressed and quietly opened his bedroom door, trying not to wake Zoe and Zach. Zoe was standing in the doorway. She threw her arms around her father's neck and said, "Be careful, Daddy, and good luck. I love you."

He slid his arms around her waist, held her tightly, and said, "Thanks, baby, I'll need it, and I love you too. Listen, this storm is supposed to be pretty bad, I may not make it back for a few days, so don't worry if you don't hear from me. Besides, this storm is a good thing. Even if Brad doesn't want me back right away, he surely wouldn't put me out in a blizzard, and then I'll have a few more days to work my magic."

"Good plan, Daddy. Don't take no for an answer," she said with a smile.

"I need to get going, honey, so I can beat the worst of the weather. I love you, and thanks for everything," Mac whispered in his daughter's ear.

"I love you too, Daddy. Be careful."

Mac quietly went downstairs, skipped the coffee, and headed straight for the front door. Before he made it down the hall, Zach caught up to him and said, "Good luck, Mr. Cleary. Zoe told me everything last night." Mac started to blush just a little.

"Thanks, Zach, but if we're gonna be related, you got to start calling me Mac."

"Good luck, Mac," he said with a smile, and gave him a hug.

FIFTEEN minutes later, Mac pulled into the Lake Hood parking lot. He checked the weather once more at his kiosk and made his way out to the dock. It was five forty-five, and daybreak was still far off. He ran through his checklist, started the engine, and requested permission to take off.

His pontoons left the Lake Hood at six ten. *That should put me at the lake by six fifty-five*, he thought. The wind was starting to pick up, but he'd flown in a lot worse. Brad was worth any chance he'd have to take to get to him and make things right.

He was in the air about thirty-five minutes and about to start his descent when his wind shear alarm sounded. The alarm indicated a possible wind shear in his immediate vicinity, so he disengaged the autopilot and took control. As he adjusted the flaps and started his descent, the winds at the lower altitudes were getting much stronger. The lower he got, the stronger the turbulence and winds became. He kept waiting to break through the low ceiling, but nothing—simply white. He immediately realized he was experiencing whiteout conditions in addition to the high winds. Mac kept a very close eye on his instruments, as whiteout conditions can produce a feeling of vertigo, where you lose the ability to determine which way is up or which way is down.

As he tried to steady the small plane and keep himself calm, he remembered the famous crash of John F. Kennedy Jr. off Cape Cod. John Jr. was flying from New York to Cape Cod and ran into a heavy fog bank. He hadn't been trained to fly with instruments alone, and combined with zero visibility, it was a disaster waiting to happen. It was later determined that the cause of the crash had indeed been vertigo.

Mac reminded himself that he was a well-trained pilot and very capable of flying on instruments alone. He knew he couldn't afford to make that mistake, but was confident that he could land the plane on the lake in the general vicinity of the lodge.

As he continued his descent, the winds became increasingly difficult to handle. He gave the engines a little more power to help push the plane through the winds, but it didn't seem to help. He was now bouncing around almost to the point that his plane was out of control. He kept waiting for a break in the snow to try and catch a glimpse of the lake, but he saw nothing but white. According to his instruments, he was about five minutes from landing when all hell broke loose. He was being blown in every direction and losing altitude quickly. He realized that he needed to get down, but he could no longer determine where he was. His last thought before he went into survival mode was, *I love you, Zoe, and God, I love you, Brad.* He flipped the switch on the radio and said, "*Mayday! Mayday!*"

chapter 31 ✈

THE winds started howling about four o'clock in the morning while Brad lay awake in bed, tossing and turning. He sighed and turned over for the umpteenth time and finally decided that he would never go back to sleep. It was now six forty-five, and he'd gotten maybe three hours of sleep the entire night. He got out of bed and stoked the fire and threw on a few more logs. The winds were already howling, two hours ahead of the forecast, and he still needed to close and secure the shutters before the worst of the storm hit.

He remembered that he'd promised Zander and Jake that he would keep his VHF radio on, so on the way to the bathroom to get dressed, he switched it on and made sure it was on channel sixteen.

Halfway to the bathroom, he stopped in his tracks. His heart stopped beating when he heard Mac's voice.

"Mayday! Mayday! Mayday! This is November 4649 Delta in the vicinity of Hiline Lake. Position: 61 degrees, 44.4 minutes north and 151 degrees, 22.9 minutes west. I'm going down. I repeat, going down. Mayday! Mayday! Mayday!

"Mayday! Mayday! Mayday! This is November 4649 Delta in the vicinity of Hiline Lake. Position: 61 degrees, 44.4 minutes north and 151 degrees, 22.9 minutes west. I'm going down. I repeat, going down."

Brad broke into a cold sweat. He ran to the radio and picked up the receiver.

"November 4649 Delta, this is Wing Mansion, do you copy?"

"Brad!" Mac yelled. "I'm going down. I'm very close to the lake, and I'm in whiteout conditions. Having trouble keeping control."

"Mac, what do I do?" Brad yelled into the radio.

"Nothing, baby, just say a prayer for me and forgive me," Mac said. "Brad, I love you, and I don't care who knows it. If I make it out of this, I will spend the rest of my life making it up to you."

Brad heard the whine of the plane's engine as it approached the cabin, then felt the vibration as it passed over, seemingly a few feet above the roof.

"Mac," Brad yelled. "You just passed over the cabin, heading away from the lake. Can you turn around?"

"Can't!" Mac shouted back. "I need to stay into the wind to help slow me down."

"I love you too, Mac. I'll find you, just don't die, Mac, please don't die," Brad begged. "Mac," he yelled. "Do you copy? Mac?" Silence.

Brad dropped the radio receiver and ran for the bathroom. He pulled on whatever clothes he could find. He slipped on one boot while hopping across the room, and he heard a very loud noise. The cabin walls shook, and he fell to the floor.

"Oh my God, Mac. Mac!" he yelled.

He crawled to the door while sliding the other boot on. He reached for a coat and a pair of snowshoes on the way out the door. He slipped the coat on as he ran, but stopped to put the snowshoes on before he started up the mountain. He ran in the direction Mac had been flying and the sound of the crash but could see very little. He didn't know what he was going to find, but he knew he had to find Mac, dead or alive.

chapter 32 ✈

BRAD knew the crash couldn't be too far from the cabin because of the force of the impact he'd felt, but where? He looked all around as he ran up the mountainside. He looked up and down for any signs of debris or a crash, but it was so hard to see anything. He ran until he couldn't run anymore and collapsed in the snow.

I've got to get up. I've got to find Mac, he thought. He rolled over in an attempt to get up, and as he looked up, he saw what appeared to be a piece of a wing from Mac's plane.

I'm so close, he thought. *I've got to keep going.*

He forced himself up and started running again. He barely kept his balance when he ran smack into a piece of the plane. It looked like part of the tail section, but he couldn't really tell. He ran farther and stopped. Through the wind, something was splashing on his head, and he looked up. What was left of the plane was lodged in the dense trees above him. He touched the liquid on his head and brought his fingers to his nose. Fuel!

I've got to get Mac out of there, he thought. *This damn thing could blow up any minute.* He looked around at the base of the trees and found one he could shimmy up. He kicked off the snowshoes and started to climb. It was difficult and slow going until he got to the first hanging limb. He used the limbs as step ladders until he made his way from one tree to the other and finally to the fuselage. The windshield was broken out, and through the opening he could see Mac slumped over the wheel, covered in snow. He shouted Mac's name. No response. He called to him again; still no response. He didn't know how much more weight the crumpled plane could handle, but he had to get to Mac.

He slowly climbed onto the nose and through the windshield as far as he could get.

"Mac, can you hear me?" he yelled. "Mac?"

Brad reached in and pushed Mac's head back, and blood was gushing out of a cut on his forehead. He felt Mac's neck and found a pulse. He was alive. Brad ripped off his coat and then his shirt. He used a piece of glass from the broken windshield and ripped off a sleeve of his shirt and tied it around Mac's bleeding head. He put his coat back on and zipped it up before he reached into the plane and released Mac's seatbelt. He attempted to pull Mac out of the seat, but his legs were jammed under the dashboard. He had to get to the seat release so he could move it back, but he couldn't reach it from his current position. He climbed all the way through the windshield and fell headfirst into the copilot's seat. Brad was able to maneuver himself into a position where he could just barely reach the release and tried to move it. It was stuck, probably from the force of the crash. He turned around to find something to use to release the seat and was surprised to see that the entire tail section of the plane was gone. He positioned himself and kicked the lever with his boot until he was able to move it and finally release the lock on the seat. Once the lock was broken, the seat flew back from Mac's weight. Brad could see that Mac's left knee was beat up pretty badly and bleeding, and Mac had a cut on his right thigh. He found a roll of duct tape in a canvas bag and wrapped Mac's knee and thigh repeatedly until the wounds were sealed. He looked around at what was left of the plane to see what he could use to get Mac down. He spotted the two cables that Mac had used to secure the plane during the last storm and decided that they were his only options.

Brad looked down to determine how far up they were, but he couldn't see the ground through the snow. He'd have to chance it and hope there was enough cable to make it down. He unwound the cable and fed one end under Mac's arms and around his chest. He secured it with the hooks attached and wrapped the other end around his waist. He pulled Mac from his seat, laid him on his back, feet first, and slid him little by little to the open end of the plane. When he was positioned at the opening, Brad braced himself between the

two seats with the cable wrapped around his waist and used his feet
to gently push Mac through the opening of the plane. Mac slid out of
the opening, and Brad felt all of Mac's weight dangling outside of
the plane. The plane started to tilt in the direction of the opening,
and Brad was thrust forward. Brad and Mac slid about three feet
before Brad caught hold again and stopped them. The plane teeter-
tottered in the treetops while he held on for dear life. He figured it
was now or never. He slowly began to lower Mac to the ground by
releasing the cable around his waist little by little and using his body
weight to secure them both. Suddenly something gave way, and the
tail dropped about two feet and stopped. Brad held his breath but
knew he couldn't panic. He had to work quickly if he was going to
get Mac to the ground. After about fifteen minutes of gently sliding
the cable around his waist, the weight and pressure were suddenly
gone.

He's got to be on the ground, Brad thought.

He removed the cable from around his waist and, not knowing
if the plane was secure enough to lower himself out the same way he
had Mac, he climbed out of the cockpit window and balanced on the
nose of the plane while he secured the other cable to one of the trees
just within his reach. He climbed back in the nose of the plane and
wrapped the secured cable around his waist. He slowly shimmied his
way through the rear opening of the plane and rappelled down until
he reached the ground. Mac was still out cold. He removed the cable
from Mac's underarms and lifted him over his shoulder. He silently
thanked himself for staying fit, and Mac for his lightweight
swimmer's build.

Brad had carried Mac for a few minutes when suddenly he
heard a loud crash, and what followed knocked them both to the
ground. What was left of the plane toppled out of the trees, hit the
ground, and exploded. The explosion engulfed the nearby trees and
continued to burn. The wind would fan the fire until all of the fuel
was gone, but everything was so wet that the fire probably wouldn't
spread.

Brad stopped every ten minutes or so to rest and then
continued on. His hands were becoming numb, and he couldn't feel

his feet, but he had Mac. He knew Mac was alive, but beyond that he had no idea what condition he was in. The going was tough, but luckily, he was going down the mountain or he would have never made it. They were still experiencing whiteout conditions, and the wind was now blowing around sixty knots, with gusts up to eighty. As they got closer, Brad picked up the pace just a little until they reached the back porch. He was exhausted, but they had made it, both alive.

Brad forced open the back door with his foot as he carried Mac to the bed. He laid Mac down and ran back to the door and forced it shut against the wind. Once back at Mac's side, he reached under the bed for his medical bag. The fire was still going, and the cabin was warm, so he removed his coat and wet boots and took Mac's pulse—weak, but steady. He removed Mac's coat and shirt and laid him back down. He unlaced his boots and removed them, along with his socks. Mac's right ankle was badly sprained and black and blue. He went to the kitchen and got a plastic bag out of the cupboard and went out back to scrape up some snow. When the bag was full of snow, he forced the door closed against the wind, and laid the bag of snow over Mac's foot.

He then removed the duct tape from both legs and surveyed the wounds. The cut on Mac's thigh was pretty deep and would require stitches. His knee was banged up pretty badly, with a couple of small lacerations, but in time would be fine. He removed his shirtsleeve from Mac's head to examine those injuries. Mac had a large trauma to the left side of his head, where he must have hit the dashboard, and a long laceration that wasn't very deep on the right, presumably from the windshield. The laceration wouldn't require stitches, but a few butterfly bandages would be required to hold it together tightly. In addition, he was sure that Mac had a pretty bad concussion, but how bad, he couldn't tell without a CAT scan or MRI.

He cleaned the head wound and made sure there were no glass particles in the laceration, then applied the butterfly bandages. He got another bag of ice, placed it on the trauma to help with the swelling, and moved on to his legs.

He gently slid Mac's pants off, trying to avoid touching the wounds and trying not to disturb his ankle. He looked through his medical bag and found a tube of topical anesthesia. It wasn't the best solution, but it was all he had and better than nothing. He decided that Mac was better off unconscious if he had to stitch him up with only topical anesthesia, but either way, Brad knew Mac would endure what needed to be done in order to recover.

Brad cleaned Mac's knee and wrapped it with gauze and an Ace bandage. He then gently cleaned the laceration on Mac's thigh. This one was very deep and would require stitches inside and outside the wound. He retrieved the surgical sutures from his medical bag and began the process. Every now and then he looked up to see if Mac was showing any signs of being in distress, but saw no change. He completed the stitches and bandaged the wound. He had done all he could for Mac here and hoped it would be enough until he could get him to the hospital.

Brad went to the radio and picked up the receiver where he'd dropped it on the floor. He pressed the button and said, "Wing Mansion to Hiline Lake Lodge, do you read?"

Static was all he heard.

"Repeating, Wing Mansion to Hiline Lake Lodge, Zander or Jake, do you copy?"

"This is Hiline Lake Lodge. Brad, is that you?"

"Zander, switch to channel three eight. Over," Brad instructed.

"Switching to channel three eight."

"Brad, are you okay? Over."

"Zander, we had an accident up here. Mac's plane went down. Over."

"What, how do you know? Over," Zander asked.

"I heard the Mayday calls on the radio and found the crash. Over," Brad said.

"We didn't hear a thing. Over," he replied. "How bad is it? Over."

"I'll explain it all later, but it's pretty bad, Zander. I was able to get Mac out of the plane before it exploded, but he's still unconscious and had several external injuries, none life-threatening. But the worst thing is that I can't tell if he has any internal injuries without a CAT scan or MRI. Over."

"What do you want us to do, Brad? Over."

"Can you use your satellite phone to get a medical airlift ASAP? Over."

"I'm right on it. I'll radio you back as soon as I can get an ETA. Over."

"Thanks, Zander. Over."

"Jake and I will be there as soon as we can. Hold tight, Brad. Over."

"Thanks, but don't take any chances. Not much we can do until we get him to a hospital. Oh, and Zander, can you call Jack and Zoe and tell them what happened and that he's alive? Over."

"Will do. Over."

"Zander, tell the airlift that I will be standing by on channel one six. Over."

"Roger that, Brad."

Brad switched the radio back to channel one six and put the handheld receiver down. He walked over to the bed and pulled back the covers from under Mac and tucked them in around him. He tried to wake him again by calling his name, but he got no response. He gently kissed him on the lips, brushed his cheek with the back of his hand, and then headed to the kitchen to start a pot of coffee. He stopped at the kitchen counter and put both his hands on the counter in front of him and bowed his head. The events of the last few hours and months started to hit him pretty hard, and he sank down to the floor and began to silently weep. When he regained his composure, he decided that he didn't want any coffee after all. He went back to Mac and climbed in bed next to him. He laid his arm over Mac's chest and closed his eyes.

Sometime later, he opened his eyes, and Mac was staring back at him with a weak smile on his face.

"It's about time you woke up, sleepyhead," Mac whispered.

"Mac, you're awake!" Brad jumped out of bed and ran around to the other side. "How do you feel?" he asked.

"I have a really bad headache, and it's difficult to breathe. What happened to me?" Mac asked.

"Your plane went down on your way here," Brad explained.

"Really?" Mac said. "I barely remember taking off."

"It's just the side effects of a concussion," Brad said. "Your memory will come back. Are you dizzy? Do you feel nauseous?"

"Not dizzy, but a little nauseous, and I'm really thirsty," Mac said.

"Take a deep breath. How bad does it hurt?" Brad asked.

Mac did as he was told. "Not too bad, just a little," he said.

"I think you have a cracked rib or two in addition to the concussion," Brad said as he ran to the kitchen to get him a glass of cool water.

"Sip it really slowly," Brad said. "Just a little at a time."

Mac took a small sip of water. He looked very confused. "The plane?" he asked.

"Totally gone," Brad said. "It's a miracle you survived. The plane was in three pieces."

Brad gave Mac two aspirin for the pain and another sip of water. He retrieved more Ace bandages from his medical bag and sat Mac up and held him there as he wrapped his chest to help his ribs and breathing.

"How did you find me?" Mac asked.

"I heard your Mayday call over the radio," Brad said. "Then I heard you pass overhead at a very low altitude, and then the cabin rumbled when you crashed. At least I knew which direction to look."

"Zoe-Grace? Did someone call Zoe?" Mac asked.

"I radioed Zander and Jake, and they called her," Brad said. "We're waiting for an airlift now."

"I don't need an airlift. I'll be fine," Mac said as he tried to sit up and fell back down.

"Mac, stay down. You have a concussion, several other external injuries, and God knows what else," Brad explained. "The worst thing is I can't tell if you have any internal injuries without X-rays, a CAT scan, or an MRI."

"Brad, really I'll be...."

Brad heard the radio come back to life.

"Wing Mansion, this is Hiline Lake Lodge, come back."

Brad ran to the radio and picked up the receiver. "This is Wing Mansion; I read you loud and clear."

"Airlift can't get here until the weather clears. Based on the latest weather report, the earliest they're saying is tomorrow morning. Over."

"I was afraid of that. I'll just have to do the best I can, Zander. Over."

"Jake and I will up there as soon as possible, and we'll figure it all out. The next problem is there's no place to land up there, so we'll need to get Mac down to the lodge. Over."

"I'll carry him down if I need to, no worries there. Over."

"Jake and I will bring up two snowmobiles, and we'll each take one back down tomorrow morning. Will he be okay to make the trip? Over."

"He'll have no choice. I'll take good care of him tonight, and hopefully he'll be okay. Over."

"We'll see you as soon as we can get up there. Over."

"Thanks, Zander. Did you get Jack and Zoe? Over."

"Yes, they were together. Jack was yelling something about Zoe reading him the riot act regarding you two. They will meet us at the hospital as soon as we give them the ETA. Over."

"Please call them back, and tell them that Mac is now conscious, talking, and seems to be okay. Over."

"Will do. Hiline Lake Lodge standing by on channel one six."

"Wing Mansion standing by on channel one six."

Brad walked back to the bed, and Mac's eyes were closed.

"Mac?"

Mac opened his eyes and smiled.

"Mac, you can't go to sleep," Brad said. "You have a concussion and need to be kept alert."

"Then talk to me," Mac said.

"Okay, for starters, what in the hell were you thinking, flying in this weather?" Brad asked. "You could have been killed."

"All I knew was that I needed to see you," Mac explained. "When I got home yesterday morning, Zoe was home early for the holidays to surprise me. She immediately picked up on something and saw that I was hurting. She pushed and pushed until I broke down and told her everything."

"Really?" Brad said. "And her reaction?"

"She was shocked to say the least, but kept an open mind, and in the end was very supportive. She told me I was an idiot for listening to Jack and for leaving you," Mac explained. "She also said I'd better get back up here and tell you how I feel before I lost you."

"Man, I like this girl already," Brad said.

"She's something really special," Mac replied. "So I thought I could beat the storm, but the weather turned on me... like sushi at a summer picnic."

Brad couldn't help himself; he started to laugh so hard he thought he would fall off of the bed.

"And," Mac said, "the rest is history."

Brad took Mac's hand and said, "If you ever do anything like this again, I will personally kill you and bury you so far under the earth, no one will ever find you, got it?"

Mac squeezed Brad's hand and said, "I love you, Brad, with all my heart, and I don't care who knows it."

"What about Jack?" Brad asked.

"Fuck Jack," Mac said with disgust. "He was supposed to be my best friend, and he made me believe I would lose my daughter and him, the only real family I have left. The funny thing is that Zoe is cool with it, and if Jack doesn't accept it, he'll be the one on the outside."

Mac took a deep breath. "Brad, I should never have left you. I should have known that Zoe would never turn her back on me. How can I ever make it up to you?"

"I love you too, Mac," Brad said. "I know you were scared and struggling, but that didn't make it hurt any less."

"I'm so sorry, Brad," Mac said. "I will spend the rest of my life, if you'll have me, making it up to you."

"Maybe just the first twenty years," Brad said. "After that, I'll probably let you off the hook."

Brad leaned down and kissed Mac on the forehead. When he was about to pull away, Mac lifted one arm and grabbed Brad behind the neck and brought their lips together for a long, passionate kiss.

"Whoa, flyboy, there will be time for that later. I need to get you well and down this mountain."

"Spoilsport," Mac said.

Brad continued talking to Mac, explaining the rescue. He went into every little detail to make the story longer, in order to hold Mac's interest and keep him from falling asleep.

After he finished the story, Mac turned his head away with tears streaming down his face.

"Mac, are you in pain? What?"

"Brad, you saved my life. Even after I turned my back on you and listened to Jack," Mac said. "You didn't know I was coming back for you."

"I kind of did know," Brad said with a sly smile.

Mac looked confused.

"You confessed your love to me over the VHF radio just before you went down. Not that it would have mattered; I took a Hippocratic oath, remember."

"I don't care what type of oath you took, I'm just happy you're here and I have a chance to make it up to you."

"Me too," Brad said. "Now you need to rest for a while."

Brad allowed Mac to sleep for short periods of time, but woke him every fifteen minutes to make sure he was okay.

Just before sunset, Zander and Jake showed up with the two snowmobiles, dinner, and a bottle of bourbon.

"I figured you might need this," Zander said as he handed Brad the bottle.

"You have no idea how bad," Brad responded.

Zander, Jake, and Brad shared the bourbon while they sat around the bed, and Brad filled them in on the rescue.

From time to time, Mac would jump into the conversation or ask a question, but for the most part, he simply rested. Finally, he reached down and rubbed his injured thigh.

"What did you do to my leg, Dr. Kildare?" he asked.

"Which one?" Brad replied.

"Both," Mac said.

"The left one needed stitches inside and out, and I didn't have anything but a topical anesthesia, but luckily, you were unconscious for that little surgery," Brad said as he rubbed the wounded leg.

"Thank God for that. I hate needles," Mac said.

"It's going to be very sore for a while," Brad assured him. "But you should heal pretty quickly."

Eventually, Zander and Jake climbed up to the loft and turned in, and Brad stripped and crawled into bed next to Mac, careful not to bump his wounds. Brad set the alarm for every half hour and felt comfortable taking short naps in between. He took Mac's hand in his and lay as still as possible until they fell asleep.

chapter 33

THE next morning they were all awakened by the radio announcing the airlift's ETA. They had more than enough time to get Mac dressed, bundled up, and down the mountain to meet the helicopter. While Zander and Jake shoveled off the front porch, Brad wrapped Mac's ankle with another Ace bandage to protect it from movement and tightened the wrapping on his chest to further secure any fractured or broken ribs. He bundled Mac up in warm clothing and threw a few things in a bag for each of them.

Mac was in good spirits, with no dizziness or nausea, sore but otherwise seemingly okay. Brad carried him to the snowmobile, went back and got his backpack, and secured it to the vehicle. They moved down the mountain very slowly, with Zander and Jake taking the lead. Brad drove with Mac tucked in tightly behind him, Mac's arms securely around his waist. Brad used one hand to steer and control their speed, while the other hand covered Mac's hands to try and hold him in place.

They reached the bottom of the mountain as the small helicopter was landing on the lake. They met the paramedics at the dock, where they moved Mac onto a stretcher.

"Do you want us to fly back with you?" Zander said, Jake standing right next to him.

"You guys have done so much already. I think I can take it from here. I don't know how we'll ever thank you though," Brad said as he hugged each of them good-bye.

Mac looked up from the stretcher and raised his hand. Zander and Jake grabbed his hand and held on for a few seconds.

"One more thing," Mac said. "Can I have my job back?"

They all laughed, and Jake said, "Of course you can."

"You'll just need a new plane," Zander added.

"I'll handle that," Mac said as they rolled him toward the helicopter with Brad in tow.

"Call us on the satellite phone as soon as you know anything," Zander shouted.

They loaded Mac into the small helicopter and strapped him in. Brad climbed in after him and buckled up as well. Zander and Jake waved them on as they lifted off the ground, heading for Alaska Regional Hospital in Anchorage.

chapter 34 ✈

ON THE tarmac at the hospital forty-five minutes later, Mac and Brad were taken in through the emergency room entrance, where they met Zoe, Zach, and Jack. Zoe ran up to the stretcher. "Daddy, are you okay? We were so worried," she said.

"I'm fine, honey," Mac said. "Do you think I'd let you get married without me there to give you away?"

Tears ran down Zoe's eyes as she hugged her father, almost climbing onto the stretcher with him.

Meanwhile, Brad glared at Jack, who turned away and looked at the ground. Zoe left her father and ran directly into Brad's arms.

"You must be Brad," she said. "Thank you for saving my father's life."

"You're welcome," Brad said.

They were interrupted by one of the paramedics. "We need to take the patient in to be examined," he said.

Brad turned to follow, but was stopped by the other paramedic. "Family only beyond this point, sir. I'm very sorry."

"He *is* family," Zoe said as she squeezed Brad's hand. "He's my father's partner."

Brad smiled at her and looked at the paramedic. "I'm also a doctor, Dr. Bradford Mitchell, Northwest Hospital, Seattle."

"Okay, Doctor," the paramedic said as he led them through the ER.

Brad went into the examining room to explain to the ER doctor what procedures he had done on Mac's head, legs, and ankle, while the rest waited in the interior waiting room.

One hour later, Brad came out of the ER and found Zoe, Zach, and Jack.

"He is a very lucky man," he said. "He's going to be fine."

Zoe again hugged him.

"He has a concussion," Brad continued, "two cracked ribs, a badly sprained ankle, two lacerations—one on his head and one on his leg—and his knee is pretty badly beaten up, but all in all, he's going to be fine. The MRI showed no internal injuries, and the X-rays showed no broken bones."

Jack stood and stepped right in front of Brad. Brad prepared himself for more of Jack's slanders, but was surprised when Jack said, "Thank you for saving Mac. I still think what you two are doing is wrong, and I'll never understand it, but you saved his life, and I will always be grateful for that."

Brad looked at Zoe and Zach with a surprised expression.

Zach stepped up and stuck out his hand. "Pleased to meet you, Dr. Mitchell. I'm Zachary Williams, Zoe's fiancé," he said. "We did our best to try and make him understand what you guys have. But he's pretty stubborn. Maybe, in time, he'll come around."

"Hey, guys?" Jack said. "I'm standing right here. I can hear every word you're saying."

"I'm glad you can hear us," Zoe said. "I haven't forgiven you yet for almost killing my father and ruining our lives in the process."

"Okay kids," Brad said. "Jack didn't want anything bad to happen to your father. He's just a bigot, that's all."

"Fine," Jack said as he turned and walked toward the doors. "Just keep the shit out of my face."

Brad looked at Zoe and Zach. "Guys, take it easy on Jack for a while. He's hurting, in his own way." Zach and Zoe looked at each other and nodded.

"When can we see Dad?" Zoe asked.

"They're going to admit him overnight for observation," Brad said. "And once they get him settled, we can all go in to see him."

In just under an hour, they were all sitting around Mac's bed, Zoe at his head on one side and Brad on the other. Brad and Zoe each had a hand, and Jack and Zach were at his feet.

"I think I'm the luckiest man alive," Mac said. "I have you guys, I survived a plane crash, and," looking at Brad, he said, "I found you."

epilogue ✈

MAC opened his eyes to the most beautiful July morning he'd ever seen. It had been seven glorious months since the plane crash, and he was completely recovered. Brad was sleeping soundly next to him. He had a new plane, and to top it all off, it was Zoe and Zach's wedding day.

Months ago he'd given his house in Anchorage to Zoe and Zach as an early wedding present, partly in hopes of luring them to practice nearby, but mostly because it was time for him to move on. He spent all of his time at the cabin with Brad, and they were truly happy there. A few months back, he and Brad had traveled to Seattle and packed up Brad's house and put it on the market. They had plans to enlarge the little cabin, but wanted to travel for a while after the wedding and see the world.

Mac thought of his and Zoe's friends, and Zach's family staying at the lodge at the base of the mountain, and how perfect this wedding was going to be for Zoe. She and Zach had made several trips to the lake over the past few months, planning out every detail, and Zander and Jake were thrilled to host the event and be involved in the planning. Brad and Zoe had become very close since the plane crash, which made Mac very happy. Jack had even come around a little, but was still struggling with something. In the end, he knew he had no choice but to accept this relationship, or he would lose his family. Jack and Brad forced a civil relationship for Mac and Zoe's sakes.

Brad moved a little, and Mac held on tighter.

"Morning, Father of the Bride," Brad said.

"Morning," Mac replied.

"How did I get so old?" Mac asked. "And when did Zoe grow up?"

"Life happens," Brad said. "Before you know it, things go and change on you."

"I know one thing that will never change," Mac said.

"What's that?" Brad said.

"My love for you," he replied. "I know it took me awhile, but I am so here now."

Brad rolled over in Mac's arms, and they were face to face.

"Mac, I never thought I would ever be happy again. You gave me a second chance, and I'm not giving that up for anything."

"I feel the same way, Brad. I love you."

"I love you too," Brad whispered. "We have to get up and get ready. We have a wedding to attend."

"Not so fast," Mac said as he rolled over on top of Brad and buried his face in Brad's neck. Brad smiled, because he knew exactly what was to follow.

SCOTTY CADE left Corporate America and twenty-five years of marketing and public relations behind to buy an inn & restaurant on the island of Martha's Vineyard with his partner of fourteen years.

He started writing stories as soon as he could read, but only recently for publication. When not at the inn, you can find him on the bow of his boat writing male/male romance novels with his Shetland sheepdog Mavis at his side. Being from the South and a lover of commitment and fidelity, most of his characters find their way to long, healthy relationships, however long it takes them to get there. He believes that in the end, the boy should always get the boy.

Scotty and his partner are avid boaters and live aboard their boat, spending the summers on Martha's Vineyard and winters in Charleston, SC, and Savannah, GA.

Visit Scotty at http://www.scottycade.com and Facebook. You can contact him at Scotty@scottycade.com.

Also by SCOTTY CADE

FINAL
ENCORE
Scotty Cade

http://www.dreamspinnerpress.com

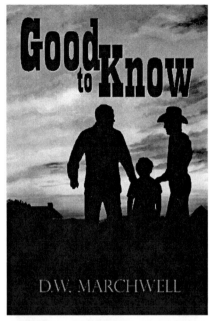

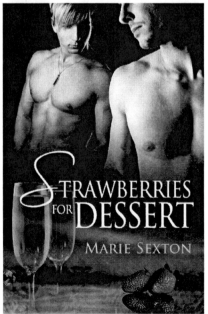

CPSIA information can be obtained at www.ICGtesting.com
265207BV00001B/4/P